JOEL

A NOVEL OF YOUNG AMERICA

by

NORA BENJAMIN KUBIE

The American Revolution is the setting for this thoughtful and exciting novel about a young Jewish refugee who comes to America in 1775 seeking the peaceful life of a scholar and escape from the persecution he has known in his native land.

Joel Davidov, conscientiously opposed to fighting and tired of violence, at first refuses to take sides in the growing Revolutionary conflict. But, unjustly imprisoned by the British, and inspired by the words and deeds of Thomas Paine and Nathan Hale, he gradually comes to a realization that he must join the colonists in their fight against tyranny and oppression.

Through the tempering effects of the war—fighting as a Minute Man as well as with George Washington in the bloody battles of New York and Connecticut—and the problems of his romance with a young Christian girl, Joel reaches maturity with a profound understanding of both his new country and himself, proud and happy to be "both an American and a Jew, with loyalty to the democratic ideals which played so large a part in both traditions."

Mrs. Kubie has written a swiftly moving story rich in description and action and full of life and meaning for the young reader of today.

Joel

Joel

JOEL

A Novel of Young America

by Nora Benjamin Kubie

Harper & Brothers

PUBLISHERS: NEW YORK

JOEL

Library of Congress catalog card number: 52-7881

". . . give ear, all ye inhabitants of the land. Did ever such a thing come to pass in your days, or ever in the days of your fathers? Tell it to your children, and let your children tell it to their children, and their children to another generation."

THE OLD TESTAMENT, BOOK OF JOEL

I wish to express my thanks to rabbis and teachers among my friends, for their advice and suggestions, and to Dr. David de Sola Pool in particular for the use of his material on Gershom Mendes Seixas.

N. B. K.

Joel

Joel

1.

April, 1775

IN MR. NATHANIEL
Shaw's warehouse by the docks at New London, Joel Davidov and the merchant's clerk, Denis Leary, had finished
checking a consignment of goods and loading it on a sloop
bound down the coast next day. Joel had been sent from
New Haven by his brother-in-law to supervise this shipment;
it was his first visit to the seaport, and he looked with curiosity
on the cluttered wharves, smelling of rum, molasses and
tarred hemp rope, and at the tall-masted vessels riding out
in the Thames.

" 'Navy of Tarshish,' " he murmured, in the old Hebrew
tongue, " 'bringing gold and silver, ivory, apes and peacocks. . . .' "

"What is that you're saying?" Denis Leary asked.

Joel laughed and repeated the Bible verse in English.

"You'll not be learning the trade if you moon on apes and

peacocks," Denis said. "You're a queer one, Red—I never saw a fellow quite like you."

Joel did not resent the remark. Both young clerks were fiery-headed, and with this as a start, they had been bantering good-humoredly all day, since the first moment of meeting. And Joel knew that other boys of seventeen here in the provinces would naturally find him strange, as different from them as the dark cramped alleyways of Warsaw were from the wind-swept marshes beyond the warehouse door. He knew he did not resemble a Connecticut Yankee, though his nose was as straight, his eyes as blue as theirs, and his well-knit frame dressed in American homespun. He was good at languages and had picked up the English words easily, but his accented speech was nothing like their Connecticut drawl. As a boy he had worked on the land; his wide shoulders and solid muscles showed it, but his skin was pale from being little out of doors. Whenever his brother-in-law Jacob's business allowed it, he still studied his books as he had done in Warsaw.

"One tells me that you Irish are peculiar too, Red," he answered Denis with a smile.

"And proud of it," Denis said. "There's nothing peculiar about hating the English king, howsomever, if that's what you have in mind. I've plenty of company here for that."

"It seems so," Joel said. "You will have to explain to me what is so bad about this English king."

Denis yawned and stretched. "That's a long, long tale, and I'll be needing something to wet my throat for the telling of it. Let's go up to the town, shall we?"

The two young men closed up the warehouse and strolled

to the street which ran along the water front. New London was a noisy place always. All day long, great wains rumbled over the cobbles with creaking wooden wheels; the whips of teamsters cracked on the patient backs of draft animals; droves of cattle, hogs and horses clattered down to the wharves. So far there had been nothing to mark this as a special day; afternoon sunshine gleaming golden on the Parade Ground saw no soldiers drilling there; the river, innocent of British ships of war, danced blue and silver to Long Island Sound. Except for the gulls, that quarreled and screamed overhead, all was peaceful.

But the galloping hoofbeats echoing through an upper street, coming to a sudden stop, were not those of a dray horse. A babble of excited voices rose in greeting, then there were cheers, and a musket shot rang out.

"A fight is it?" Denis cried delightedly. "Or what would the excitement be?"

He broke into a run, and Joel followed him to the tavern, where a crowd pressed thick around a man who stood gulping a flagon of ale while a hostler rubbed down his streaming horse.

" 'Tis a messenger on his way to New York," an onlooker told Denis. "He just come a-galloping in from Boston with big news."

"We gave the Lobsters more than they looked for," the messenger said, wiping the foam from his lips. "They didn't find Mr. Adams nor Mr. Hancock, nor the ammunition stores they was after, no siree! They got gunpowder and lead all right—in the seat of their pants. I tell you, the war's begun, boys!"

3

Although there had been discontent in the Colonies for some time, until this day there had been nothing that you could call a battle. But now at Concord and at Lexington, the militia had stood up against the British Regulars; men had been wounded and killed on both sides—more Redcoats than Provincials, Praise God. According to the messenger, the King's men had been badly whipped.

A man threw his cap into the air. Another looked at him sourly. "This ain't going to be a picnic to shout huzza for. Mebbe they caught the Royal Governor, Mister Gage, napping this time, but he won't let it rest there. From now on any man who sticks up for his rights will be putting his neck in the noose."

The messenger rode on his way, and soon the streets were swarming as his story spread from house to house and was carried to farmers in outlying districts. In the midst of the cheering and the speeches which were going on in a dozen places at once, Joel was silent and perplexed, but Denis was shouting with the rest and flourishing his fists.

"Denis, Denis," Joel said, trying to quiet him down, "think on this, my friend. The way of violence—it is not good!"

"It's the only way you'll ever win an argument with the English," Denis answered.

But he followed Joel into a side street, arguing as he walked, till a crowd of workmen and sailors swept from around the corner, dragging an old gentleman in their midst. Urchins squirmed under the elbows of the older rowdies to poke and pinch the victim, and shouted, "Down with the Tories! Down with the Tories!"

4

Joel had heard of these toughs who called themselves by the high-sounding name—"Sons of Liberty." Pretending to convert Loyalists, they looted houses, frightened women, and sometimes rode a man out of town on a rail. Joel, newly come to the country, did not understand why they did it; such carryings on seemed to have little to do with liberty.

There was even a girl with them this time, a young demon with her cap crooked on a tangled mop of white-blond hair, who danced and darted in a swirl of calico skirts. Trying to hold her back was a boy like enough to be her brother. "Please, Abby, please come away," he was saying, "our uncle will be angered with you for such behavior."

"Pooh to our uncle!" the girl cried. "The old Malignant deserves to be given a good scare—everyone knows it!"

Whatever the old gentleman had done, Joel could not bear to hear the quavering voice that begged for mercy, the whimpers of pain. He had heard this sound before, in the streets of Warsaw. He had seen old Jews with patches of beard torn out, with faces sorrowful and resigned, scholars and gentle people, some of them his own relatives or his father's friends. His skin crawled with a rash of hatred he had known as a child when, cowering at the window, he had witnessed scenes like this.

He pushed his way into the mob. "What do you make with the poor old man?" he cried. "What has he ever done to be treated so?"

The old gentleman looked like a half-dead fledgling bird, with shrunken limbs and bald skull from which the wig had been torn.

"What's it to *you*?" cried one of the toughs, a tall fellow

5

with a long blue chin and a mouth lean and hungry as a shark's. "D'you believe in licking the King's boots, too?"

"No, I don't lick boots," Joel said.

"You're some kind of furriner though, by your lingo," the man said. "Why don't you go back to your own country? We can manage our affairs without advice from them what don't belong here." He reached out a dirty paw and ripped the sleeve from the old gentleman's coat.

"That's telling him, Alf," said another. "That's showing him! A coat of tar and feathers instead of his pretty velvet will mebbe cure the squire of his taste for English tea!"

Joel's anger boiled up in him hotter than a tea brew. Hardly knowing what he did, he knocked the dirty paw away and stepped squarely between the old Tory and his tormentor. "I say you should leave him alone!" he shouted.

The man Alf looked at him astonished, glaring like a bull brought up short. He swung at Joel and missed, too full of wine for aim. Suddenly Joel was surrounded; all he could see was a forest of threatening fists, some clutching belaying pins, butchers' cleavers, or the knives used for gutting fish. This time he'd brought something on himself from which escape would be hard. Though his arms were pinned to his sides by the mob, he twisted this way and that, kicking viciously at shins. He'd leave a few bruises at least, and, if he could only get his hands free, some marks on those grinning faces before he went under.

Somewhere a bell began to clang, and as it continued, man after man lost interest in the fight and went off to see what the summons meant. Only three were left; two trying to hold the squirming Joel, while the third, the one called Alf,

6

delivered a hobnailed kick in the stomach which left Joel doubled up in pain. They would have finished him off then, but Denis waded into the fight like a wiry, redheaded fury. Not liking the punishment he was handing out, two of them extricated themselves and slunk off down the street. The third, Alf, drew back and made a mock bow to the young girl who, frightened but fascinated, had stood watching. "Well, Missy, fancy seeing *you* here helping me to confound the gentry! Your Pa wouldn't like that much, would he?"

The girl crimsoned with anger at his impudent tone, turned her back on him, and retreated to her brother's side. The man laughed, and then he too walked away. The old Tory was leaning against a house wall, sick and trembling. The girl took a step toward him, and Joel caught a flash of involuntary pity in her hazel eyes, framed in long lashes and eyebrows that were startlingly dark under her pale mop of silky hair. Only a momentary flash of pity, and then she picked up her skirts and fled like a deer, with her brother panting after her.

When the old gentleman had been helped to his doorstep, Joel and Denis also followed the sound of the bells to the courthouse on the Parade, where the doors had been flung open for a meeting.

"So you don't believe in violence, eh, Joel?" Denis grinned. "After watching you, I'd like to see the day you *do* be believing in it, and I hope it's not on the wrong side you'll be then, like just now. If it hadn't been that I know the Tories deserve what they're getting, I'd have loaned you a hand much sooner; fighting's second nature and a pleasure to me. Who ever heard of a redhead that was a man of peace?"

7

Joel did not answer. His temper was a trial; he was ashamed of it. For all that he read in the books about patience and tolerance, for all that he tried to school himself in these virtues, his temper was always getting him into scrapes. There were some things a man couldn't be expected to stand. He thought bitterly of the remark, "Why don't you go back to your own country?" He had no country. He could not go back to Poland, nor did he want to. Poland was finished, destroyed. And the ancient land of Israel was in the hands of the Turks.

He had hoped to make this British colony his country. Here in Connecticut, liberty seemed to flourish as in no other part of the globe. Here a man—even though he was a Jew—could go where he wished and work as he pleased. But his Yankee neighbors were always growling about oppression. Why, *they* did not know what the word meant; they had never seen men tortured and murder done in the name of a king. The things they grumbled over were trifles; they named it tyranny because taxes cut into the profits of their trading, because a few soldiers of the King were quartered in Boston. Joel felt they should instead be grateful, as he was, for the many good things here.

He looked around him in the courtroom. Latecomers were still trying to crowd inside, pushing so that Joel half fell against the occupant of the bench before him. He murmured an apology and saw that it was the girl Abby. She gave her brother a poke. "Look—behind me—it is the one who tried to rescue Squire Weeks from the Sons of Liberty," she hissed.

"Hush, Abigail," her brother said. "Have you no manners

8

at all? One would never know you were a well-brought-up Puritan maid."

"I have manners—but it's so much fun to forget them," she said, with mischief in her voice. Then in a whisper, but loud enough so Joel heard, "He has courage—for a Tory-lover."

"When our mother learns that you all but took part in a street brawl, she will certainly chastise you, and me too," the "I have a weakness for the wine of Curaçoa myself," the she may say that if he did not have the sense to keep you within doors on a day like this—when there are scoundrels like Alf Hodges roaming the streets—I should have! I wonder how that lazy thieving rascal chanced to be in New London?"

"I suppose he couldn't find any handy work to do in Fairfield after Papa dismissed him," the girl said. "I do wish he weren't a Son of Liberty; that makes him on our side. It is a glorious day for the cause, just the same, and I would not have missed the excitement. If you had locked me in, I should have climbed out of the window to see it." She sighed windily. "If only I were a man, I would go right off to Boston to fight."

"That is for me to do," her brother said. "Let us return to Uncle's house now, Abby, before there is more trouble." He tugged at her hand, but she would not rise.

Joel had never seen a girl like this one. A Jewish maiden of fourteen would never behave so. Still he found her bold ways engaging, like those of a high-spirited puppy. Now she straightened her dimity cap and folded her hands in her apron so that one would never have recognized the earlier hoyden, except for a few rebellious blond curls that she had not quite managed to tuck away. "I will be good, Abner, I promise," she told her brother. "Only let me stay to hear the speechifying."

These Yankees, Joel thought, were great fellows for "speechifying." One after another was leaping to his feet to denounce the King, the King's governors, the King's generals, the King's soldiers. No one in the hall knew for sure who had fired the first shot at Lexington, Redcoat or Rebel, but it did not seem to matter to these people. It was enough to know that farmers and workers like themselves, armed with old fowling pieces and led by officers they themselves had chosen, had sent the British Regulars back to Boston with their tails between their elegant legs.

At first there were still a few in the hall who thought that if only the King's ear could be reached, he would right their wrongs, do away with the restrictions on trade, send Governor Gage and his garrison packing. Had not the King often called the Colonists his *loyal* and *beloved* subjects?

These moderates were quickly booed down. Almost every able-bodied man in the hall was eager to march to the aid of his comrades in the Massachusetts Bay Colony. A show of force, they cried, was the only way to bring George the Third and his councilors to terms.

The rowdies on the benches quieted when a young man arose to speak. He looked to be about twenty, only three years older than Joel himself. He was tall and well-built, with soft light hair and very fair skin. For all of his fiery words, there was gentleness in his well-cut mouth, intelligence in his fine eyes.

" 'Tis the schoolmaster from the Academy," Denis whispered. "Everybody loves him—the girls too, they say. His name is Nathan Hale."

Outside the courthouse, the April afternoon was burning away into sunset. A shaft slanting through a western window struck the platform where Nathan Hale stood and added its glow to his earnest face. He pleaded for action at once. Eloquently he quoted classics and passages from the Old Testament.

"Even he thinks it's come to a fight, and him studying to be a parson," Denis said. "Let's join up together, Red—you and me could lick the stuffing out of any Englishman."

Uncomfortably Joel shook his head. Teachers and scholars, he thought, and particularly men of God, should lead the people to peace, as long as there was a chance that there could be peace with justice. It was a pity that Nathan Hale, so ardent and persuasive, did not see this. He seemed convinced that the cause could only be won through bloodshed; he went even beyond the speeches of the others. "Let us organize and drill as we march," he said, "and never lay down our arms until we have obtained our independence!"

From all parts of the hall, men were pushing forward. Denis was soon lost amongst them. Abner had deserted his sister's side; even the man Alf was volunteering. Joel edged his way instead toward the door at the back. As he slipped out, he caught a last glimpse of Abigail, twisting in her seat to watch him go. He thought he detected a look of scorn on the small red mouth. Joel flushed angrily. Why should he care what a harum-scarum Gentile moppet thought of him?

Outside it was already dark, and the bare elm boughs

11

stood against the night sky like gibbets. Joel tramped across the cobbles and down the river bank to the quiet, deserted wharves.

Was it not more important, he thought, to study the wisdom of the ages, to search for the way toward greater happiness for all men, than to plunge into reckless impatient action? Nathan Hale, himself a scholar, did not think so. And he had called for more than action—for complete independence.

Independence—that could be achieved only by revolution. Joel Davidov knew the cost of revolutions. The Poland of his boyhood had been one long succession of uprisings and civil wars. Even as a child he had seen the Czarina's Cossacks riding through the villages, massacring Catholics and Jews. As a student in Warsaw, Joel himself had been a follower of Count Pulaski, who wished to assassinate the King and set Poland free.

He remembered coming home after a day of rioting in the streets with his fellow students to the walled-in courtyards of the Ghetto, and the tiny dark room which his ailing mother struggled to keep neat and clean. A bare and shabby room save for the seven-branched brass candlestick and the many books that had been his father's. The stone basement walls were thick, but through the small window came the sad, melodic chanting of the Talmudists in a House of Study nearby. His mother's dark eyes were pleading and frightened. "Joel—Yosele—" she had said, "you are a good boy; you love learning; perhaps one day you will be a rabbi. Do not mix with those who make revolution. You will be killed like your father, who thought he could speak up against a Cossack."

"Must we always be kicked and beaten then, Little Mother?" he had asked. "Must we be killed and imprisoned always for no reason but that we are Jews? Must we always allow it so patiently? If we stand together and fight, some day we will win."

She shrugged her thin shoulders. "What matters, who wins? Everything will happen again, as it always has. This Pulaski—this wonderful leader you speak of—he is not a Jew, so why should he care what becomes of us?"

"He wants Poland to be free," Joel said slowly.

She shrugged again. "Free Poland—no free Poland! *We* suffer as much under one name as the other. Better we say nothing and walk softly. This only is how we Jews have managed to live, since Jerusalem."

Joel often wondered if his mother had been right. The rebellion had failed; its leaders killed or driven into exile; many more poor people had been massacred, and he himself had fled to America. Perhaps the way of violence was bound to fail. Now his mother was dead, and he had joined his sister and her husband in the town called New Haven. The very name of it seemed like a good omen. All he desired was a haven where he would be let alone, to do the day's work in his brother-in-law's store, and in the evenings to study his books or wander down by the shore when the books gave no answers to his questioning. And now he sought the lonely darkness of the wharves, hoping the quiet lapping of the water and the fresh salt breeze would soothe the puzzled fever in his brain.

But at the sound of his footsteps, a voice hailed him, a Yankee voice echoing hollowly from the harbor depths. "That you, Seth?"

Joel was startled but when he saw the pale reflection of an oil lamp, he remembered that the coasting sloop, on which Jacob's goods were loaded, was tied up at the foot of the wharf. He walked toward it. "This is Joel Davidov," he called in answer.

"That boy of mine went off to join the fun and I ain't seen hide nor hair of him since," Captain Barry said. "I'll bet my sea boots he's volunteered for a soldier, leaving me shorthanded."

"Maybe not, maybe he comes back by morning," Joel suggested.

"I wasn't aiming to wait till morning to sail," the captain said.

Joel looked down at the waist of the sloop piled with cases and hogsheads, and thought, why should he not go to New Haven by boat, along with the consignment of goods? "If you will take me, Captain, I would be glad to help. You would have to tell me what to do, of course; I do not know much of boats."

The captain stared at Joel. His lean wind-reddened face was doubtful. "Thought you said you was going back to New Haven by coach."

"I had so intended; I had not thought of this. I should like it very much if you would take me." He tried to mask his eagerness, for it did not pay to appear overanxious.

Captain Barry held the lantern up to Joel's face so that he blinked. There was a long uncomfortable silence. The captain turned his back, busying himself with some ropes. After a moment, he said gruffly, "Where do you stand, boy? For or against the import taxes?"

"This is not my business because I do not understand it," Joel answered. "It is only a few months since I arrived here —from Europe."

The captain grunted. "I don't care a hoot where you come from, or what breed of beast you are so long as it ain't a king-lover. You're clerk to Jacob Peretz in New Haven? That's in your favor. He does his bit, quiet like."

Joel, puzzled, looked questioningly at the captain. "I only want to sail with you to New Haven," he repeated. "If I can help, it will be so much better."

Matt Barry glanced impatiently at his silver turnip watch. "I may be a dang fool but I'm inclined to take a chance on you." He beckoned to Joel to jump down from the pilings to the deck. He loosened the stern line and the sloop swung out into the stream, straining at the hawser which still held its nose to the wharf. "Tide's turned already," the captain said. "With this wind, I could have got off an hour back if it hadn't been for that rascal Seth!"

Joel frowned, staring out into the darkness. He wondered why the captain couldn't wait till morning to sail. Surely it was more difficult to navigate by night than by day.

2.

THE little vessel ghosted
silently away from the lights and voices of the town, down
river past the yellow reflections of the oil lantern in the light-
house tower on the western bank. It was a clear starry night
with an offshore breeze bringing the smell of salt marsh and
moist spring earth long after they had cleared the mouth of
the Thames. Matt Barry sat at the helm, undisturbed by
the reefs which stuck their heads above water like dark
plums in milk pudding. Obviously he knew his way as well
as if it were broad daylight.

Joel's spirits rose as the sails lifted and filled with the
freshening breeze. When he had taken ship after the dark
days in Warsaw, the sea with its endless horizons spoke to
him of freedom such as he had never known. Now the very
smell of salt water brought back this feeling.

In New Haven where he had come to live with his sister,
he had met for the first time a new kind of man to him,

16

neither peasant nor aristocrat. Men like Matt Barry, whose face, in the light of the lantern by the binnacle, was hard and wind-bitten but not unkind—the face of one who captained his own ship and would knuckle under to no one.

The mainland had disappeared in darkness astern. Matt Barry set a course along the Sound, narrowed his eyes, and stared into the night. Joel could make out nothing but the gently breathing black water, could hear nothing but the hiss of bubbles sliding by the hull. Barry grunted as if satisfied, sat down and lit his pipe with a paper spill from the lantern.

"There was so many scalawags about, I couldn't leave my ship even to hear the speech making," he said. "Did you listen, young fellow? What did you make of it?"

"I thought—they do not know what it is to have a war or they would not boast so over what they will do," Joel answered.

" 'Pears like you don't understand, being a stranger, what we're up against," Matt Barry said. "A man fights for what he believes in, don't he?"

"If he is sure that is the only way to get it. What is it you feel you must fight for—here in Connecticut Colony?"

"Here in Connecticut we've a charter and we won't stand for King George taking it away like in Massachusetts. All them Boston folk done was dump some tea overboard rather than pay taxes the King put on it. We've had some tea dumping here too, I can tell you, and anyone who drinks English tea, I know he's my enemy."

So that was what the Sons of Liberty had against the old Tory.

"I believe that men has a natural right to govern themselves," Matt Barry went on. "No king across the water is going to tell *us* what we should do."

"I believe this is important too," Joel said thoughtfully. "But with patience—and slowly—cannot one get such things without war? In Poland I saw what happened when one side began the killing—there was much blood spilled of innocent people." He sighed. "I do not wish to kill my fellow man."

"None of us do," Matt Barry said. "Sometimes it can't be helped. You're mighty patient for a young chap who should have red blood in his veins. *I* say, more power to those at Lexington who wouldn't let the King's men take their powder or captivate Mr. Adams and Mr. Hancock—they'd a right to speak up for our side. We'll send Boston help, and we'll see that it don't happen to us."

"Schoolmaster Hale spoke of independence," Joel said.

"We-ell, I don't know as I'd go as far as that—not yet, leastways. I'll be loyal to the Crown, so long as it don't interfere with my honest business."

Just what was Matt Barry's business this particular night? Joel knew of no cargo for Jacob which should make the captain keep so sharp a watch on every side. If, after all, he was in fear of rocks or shoals, why had he chosen to sail at night? But one did not ask too many questions of these shrewd suspicious Yankees, no matter how friendly they seemed.

The captain knocked out his pipe, and a shower of sparks sizzled into the water. "Seems like a long time since dinner. Join me in a snack, young fellow?"

In spite of his interest in books and things of the spirit, there was nothing ascetic about young Joel; he had a lusty

18

appetite. He offered eagerly to fetch the food if the captain would tell him where it was stowed.

"I'll get it myself," Matt Barry said, shortly. "Don't like folks rummaging in my cabin. You take the tiller—even a landlubber couldn't do much harm in this steady breeze."

Joel tried to keep the bow headed for the star which Captain Barry had pointed out as a guide, but the bright twinkle seemed to swing from one side of the sky to the other. The sloop quivered and struggled as if it were a live animal, and left a trail of phosphorescence astern that looped and zig-zagged. Matt Barry, returning, said, "Steady, lad—not so heavy handed. My *Amantha* has to be treated delicate, like a fine filly." Cutting off a slice of cheese with his knife and a slab of bread to go with it, he handed them to Joel and sat down again at the helm. "You'd catch the hang of it after a while if I showed you, but we've no time to meander in circles this night." He took a swallow of ale and offered the jug to Joel. "You like working for Mr. Peretz, the Jewish merchant?"

"Jacob Peretz is my sister's husband. I am a Jew also," Joel said.

"That so? I'd never have took you for one. No offense meant, you understand. Most Hebrews I've seen is little and dark and Spanish-appearing."

"If they come from Spain, they look that way often—just as I come from Poland, near the Russian border, and people take me sometimes for a redheaded Russian peasant. But I am not one, inside."

"Well then, if you stay here long enough, mebbe you'll grow a Yankee look," the captain said.

19

The tide flowing in from the open ocean at the eastern end of the Sound raised a following sea in which the sloop wallowed with creaking spars and sails slatting. "Don't mind the motion, do you?" Matt Barry said curiously.

"It makes one sleepy, like a cradle rocking," Joel said.

"You seem to relish this like you was born to it," the captain said. "Been around ships a good bit?"

"The ship I came to this country in was the first I ever saw. But I liked it so very much, I borrow little boats to row myself in at New Haven, in the harbor there, every chance I can."

"Curious—I never figured Hebrews as sailors," Barry said. "Just like I never figured any of 'em was blue-eyed, like you."

"But, Captain, surely you read in the Scriptures of the first sea captain?" Joel asked with a grin.

"Who's that?"

"Noah, of course."

Matt Barry laughed. "Reckon the first whaler was one of you too—Jonah, I mean."

Joel stretched out on the deck and watched the topmast swaying against the bright powdered arch of the Milky Way till he could no longer keep himself awake. "You will tell me when you need help?" he said drowsily. "If you would like for me to steer perhaps?"

"I got to keep my weather eye peeled," the captain said. "The wind is dropping—the very thing I was afeared of."

To Joel's inexperienced eye, the calmness of the sea was comforting; the clear and glittering sky gave no hint of weather to be afraid of. It should be a beautiful day tomorrow.

He slept deep and long in spite of the hard deck, and woke to hear Matt Barry swearing. The wind had freshened again; purple wavelets reflected the pale coral sky of dawn. The long dark knife edge of Long Island cut between the water and the sunrise, and against it stood the blue silhouette of a ship. Foam burst before its bow and streamed in white ribbons along its sides. It was bearing down on them.

Matt Barry was staring at it; a muscle twitched at the corner of his lean jaw.

"What kind of a ship is it?" Joel ventured to ask.

"Dunno yet—whatever she be, she's too dang curious," he said.

Now one could see long sleek lines built for speed, and a topmast raking the dawn sky. The lip of foam at the bow gave the oncoming ship a white grin of triumph.

"Mind your jib sheets, boy!" Captain Barry yelled, "I'm going to show that thief-looking crew a clean pair of heels to windward." He swung the tiller over and headed back toward the Connecticut shore.

The little sloop, struggling into the teeth of the wind, thrusting through the choppy waves, buried its nose and flung back salt flood from which the ice of winter had barely vanished. Water ran down the decks and sluiced through the scuppers; Joel, clinging to slippery shrouds, scrambling to carry out half-understood orders, expected each moment to be washed overboard.

Again and again Matt Barry altered his course and the larger ship copied him. Each time he came about, the cutter, with its greater expanse of sail, cut down his lead. "I'm making for the Thimbles," Barry shouted above the whistling wind. "Reefs there that a stranger mought not know." Cords stood out on the arms that gripped the tiller; his eyes watched the sail for the slightest flutter. Joel skidded from rail to rail at each tack, fighting the wind as he hauled in the slapping jib.

The captain was measuring the distance between the two vessels with narrowed eyes, biting his lips; his face was grim. "British Revenuer, or I miss my bet," he muttered. "Dang it, I didn't figure on their patrolling so far from Boston." The ship was crowding on sail: a topsail and a jib-topsail too. On it came, a mass of taut canvas towering pink in the sunrise, with the blood-red ensign of St. George streaming from the masthead.

A riffle of shoal water broke the smooth blue ahead, and the deeper blue mass of shore line was separating into headlands and small rocky islands, each with its covey of black reefs. In that maze of tricky passages, only a native and an expert could find the channel; the Britisher would rip itself apart should it dare to follow. But the water between the two vessels was narrowing rapidly. Joel could already hear shouted commands aboard the cutter and the rattle of blocks as she came about to copy each one of Captain Barry's maneuvers.

"They're getting us, burn them!" Matt Barry said. He braced himself against the side and with bulging muscles, took in another inch on the close-hauled mainsail. "Trim in that jib, boy!"

The rough, salt-encrusted line burned Joel's palms; the boat shuddered and shook. White froth of a reef's edge slid by scarcely a foot away. Another hundred yards and they'd be safe.

The dull boom of cannon shot sounded above the wailing wind and the rushing water. The British cutter had unleashed its swivel gun.

Matt Barry snapped the tiller hard over and came about again, dodging and zigzagging. Rocky ledges, pocked with barnacles and bearded with seaweed, lurked under their lee, and shots fell splashing all around, so close that one could feel the breeze of their passing. Joel, with clenched fists and tight throat, strained and quivered with each quiver of the hunted boat. Only fifty yards to go now to reach the shelter of the islands.

And then a crash and a scream like that of a wounded creature. An iron ball had struck the mast squarely; it leaned, hung for a moment in mid-air, and toppled slowly into the sea, dragging with it a mass of heavy canvas and tangled shrouds. The sloop lurched over on its beam-ends.

Matt Barry scarcely gave the shambles a glance. "Get below on the jump," he ordered, pushing his way through the debris. "I've stuff to get rid of before them Britishers board us."

He ripped up the floorboards of the after cabin and loaded Joel with demijohns of dark-colored glass to be pitched overboard. Before he could bring up a second load, a shallop was alongside with a crew of armed seamen.

Matt Barry's face was a picture of respectable indignation as he demanded to know from the officer in charge why his peaceful trading vessel, going about its legal business, should be attacked, his property thus gravely damaged.

"Let's have a look at your cargo," the officer said.

Matt Barry produced the bill of lading which Joel had

23

helped to draw up. "Sugar, molasses and rum from New London to New Haven," he said. "Coastwise trade and all strictly legal goods. Would you care for a noggin of rum, sir?"

The officer paid him no heed but ordered the casks on deck to be broken open. With hatchet, cutlass and belaying pin, the staves and barrel heads were smashed till the deck was streaming and sticky. "Make a thorough search below," the officer ordered.

They waited in anxious silence while from the cabin came the sound of boxes and casks being ripped apart, and finally of the floorboards, which Matt Barry had replaced, being taken up again. "What's this?" the British officer demanded when a sailor appeared on deck with a demijohn under each arm.

"Dutch spirits, sir," Matt Barry said. "I carry a bit of it for myself and my friends that favor it. You wouldn't call that carrying contraband, would you?"

"I have a weakness for the wine of Curaçao myself," the officer said. "I'll accept your offer of a drink now if I may."

Matt Barry took a demijohn, made a show of struggling to open it, pretended to slip in a pool of molasses, lost his balance and staggered against the side, loosing his grip on the bottle, as he did so, and letting it drop overboard as if by chance. He swore at his own clumsiness.

"Why did you bother to pull a cork, my Yankee friend?" the Englishman drawled. "Can we not drink the whole bottle before the day is up if we are to be friendly?" He swung the second demijohn against the rail, and a stream of black grains poured from the shattered neck. "As I thought—gunpowder!! Gunpowder for the Rebels, eh?"

Matt Barry shrugged. " 'Tis not what I was told the contents would be. Is it my fault that there are dishonest shippers?"

"You'll find out soon enough that it is!" the officer snapped, ordering the two rebels to be tied up and taken to the Revenue cutter.

From its deck they saw the seamen hack away the splintered mast of the sloop and then turn their hatchets against the trim hull. Matt Barry's face went first crimson and then white. "Blast you! You've no right to do that to a man's private property!"

Right or no, he was a bound and unarmed prisoner against the might of His Majesty's Navy. The scuttled wreck that had been his pride, filled, settled and plunged to the bottom, leaving only a mass of scum and debris, and the torn sails floating on the surface like a great wounded gull. Matt Barry groaned.

Then, without further parley, the prisoners were thrust into the hold and the hatch cover battened down above them. It was black as night, airless and sour smelling. Joel felt his way along the slimy timbers to a heap of old sacking, and there he stretched out, unhappy and bewildered by this turn of fortune. Overhead on the deck there were pounding feet, the rattle of block and tackle, and the slap of canvas. "Getting under way," said Matt Barry, and again he groaned. "I've sneaked in many a load of powder under the nose of the British. I calculated the risk was worth it—but I should have warned you, lad, before I let you come."

"I begged you to take me," Joel said. "Anyhow it is too

late now for being sorry. What will they do with us, do you think?"

"I dunno," Matt Barry said gloomily. "For me it could be the gallows. Or Old Mill Prison in England, which they say is worse than hanging. It's a living death. . . ."

His voice dwindled off into the darkness and for a while there was no sound but the groaning of the ship's timbers, the piping of the wind in the shrouds above, the monotonous sound of a keg not properly lashed which rolled back and forth, back and forth, as Joel himself was rolling with the motion of the vessel.

"Feel that swell?" Matt Barry said. "We'll be going out around Orient Point to the ocean—looks like it's England we're bound for, sure enough." There was a long silence. Then Matt Barry said, in a voice meant to be reassuring, "When it comes to trial, lad, they'll have to believe me that you're innocent of all this."

"I am not afraid," said Joel. But he was glad the darkness hid his face. He knew that the queasiness he felt was not the result of the motion and the odor of the hold, but because he neither wanted to die nor to languish in jail. Especially for a misdeed of which he had had no knowledge, for a cause that was not his own.

Well, it did very little good to try to keep out of trouble as his mother had advised. He bowed his head and prayed silently that he would be able to take whatever came with the courage and dignity of his father and his father's father, of all his people, who were no strangers to trouble.

3.

THE prisoners stood on deck, dizzy and blinking at the dazzling sunpath which led across the water to long wharves and a town sprawling upward on bold hills. Sunlight glinted from a golden cock atop one of the many church steeples and touched the white wings of gulls wheeling above white sails in the harbor.

The air was clean and fresh after the stale odors of the hold, and everything seemed to speak of freedom.

"Boston town," Matt Barry told Joel. "Praise be, we're still on the right side of the ocean."

But they soon found it made little difference what side of the ocean they were on, since Boston was ruled by a British governor. Matt Barry was marched off and that was the last Joel saw of him. He himself was taken to the Provost of Boston, a huge man, bloated with drink, bulging from the chair in which he lounged. Before him Joel stood, swaying,

27

weak with weariness and lack of food, while the questions buzzed around his ears like stinging yellow jackets.

"What was your part in the treason?"

"I didn't know of any treason," Joel protested.

"Who planned this affair?" the Provost asked.

Joel did not know what to say. Perhaps the New London merchant Nathaniel Shaw had planned it, or perhaps even his own brother-in-law Jacob. It was safer to say nothing. He merely shrugged. A deputy, standing by, cuffed him across the face. "Answer his Honor!"

"I don't know anything!" Joel said, his anger rising.

"How did that pernicious Yankee caitiff press you into service?" the Provost demanded.

"He didn't press me into service," Joel said.

"Aha! Then you *did* join him willingly!"

"I was a passenger," Joel said, but almost before the words were out of his mouth, the deputy struck him again, and cursed him for a blackhearted liar. No matter what he said before this court of Inquisition, it would be held against him or twisted to incriminate Matt Barry.

"Well," said the deputy, "are you going to speak up, or ain't you?"

Joel licked his bruised lips and was silent.

"Put him in the Black Hole," said the Provost. "He'll come to his senses there, I warrant."

The Black Hole was a dungeon. "You'll be hanging from the gallows in the morning," the deputy said, as he clamped a pair of manacles on Joel's wrists and delivered another blow which sent him sprawling on the slimy floor. He added that the prisoner might have a priest if he desired. "Better ask your God for mercy—and make a clean breast of what you done before you die."

"My God knows what is in my heart," Joel retorted. "Nor do I have sins that would interest the Provost, if that's what he is after."

The trap door clanged to overhead. The place smelled of the graveyard; stone walls sweated moisture, rats scampered in the darkness, and vermin crawled over him. With chained wrists, he could not drive them away. The minutes seemed hours at first and then they began to race as he realized he had little time left for living. Then again his fear was swept aside by rage, and he banged his manacled fists against the floor, and pictured what he would do to the Provost if he could.

When the trap door opened, Joel painfully straightened his back and stretched his cramped limbs. So the time had come to die. Well, he would show them he was not afraid.

At the top of the steps, the turnkey stood waiting. The noblehearted Provost, he told Joel, had taken mercy on him and put off the hanging for the time being. Roughly he unlocked the manacles, yanked them off, and shoved Joel into a cell. Pale morning light from a high-barred window filtered down on some poor creatures that were mere bundles of rags huddled on straw pallets. At the clang of the closing cell door, a few of them stirred and muttered a curse at being awakened. One of them, an old fellow who said his name was Patrick (but he'd forgotten the rest of it), sat up and asked Joel if it was thievery or drunkenness for which he'd been brought in.

"They have only false charges against me," Joel said.

29

Patrick grunted; that was what everyone pretended when they first came. He himself could not remember what he was supposed to have done—it had been so long ago.

The odor of new-baked bread drifted in on the morning breeze through the cell window. It made Joel's nostrils quiver and his stomach contract, but the daily ration of moldy crusts was not handed in till afternoon. To quench his thirst he was directed to a bucket in a corner of the cell. There was little water left, and what there was of it was warm and foul, for the bucket was filled only once in each twenty-four hours. When it was used up, the prisoners did without.

For weeks time dragged so wearily that it was hard to thank God for being alive. All he could see of the world was the small patch of sky outside the window, sometimes blazing blue, sometimes cold and gray. At night it would be a shade less black than the window frame, or powdered with stars, and each month the moon would trace a pattern, striped with bars, on the stone floor of the cell. Joel was the only one of the prisoners who cared to keep track of the days. Each morning, when he had made his prayer, he scratched a mark on the wall. The phylacteries, which he had bound on brow and hand when he prayed as ordered in the Scriptures, had long since been taken away.

He asked the jailer for a Bible. "The gentleman lodging with us that wants special privileges pays for them," the man said. And he added craftily, "For a reasonable sum, I could even give you back them little leather boxes you speak to your God with." But Joel's pockets had long since been rifled of money too, and he had no friends in Boston to pay for his comforts, as, according to the jailer, some of the prisoners did.

One day, instead of the usual stale bread, chunks of gray, greasy meat were tossed in through the cell door. Wild with excitement, the prisoners fought for them like a pack of hungry dogs; Joel snatched up a piece and was about to tear it apart with his teeth when he saw what sort of meat it was.

The jailer spied him standing with the salt pork in his hand, and a look of bitter disappointment on his face. "Ain't it good enough for you, my fine young master?"

"It is *trefa*—unclean," Joel answered in a low voice.

"Well, if it ain't clean enough for a dirty Jew like you, you'll just have to starve," the man said cheerfully.

If, for a moment, hunger had tempted Joel to break the dietary laws, the keeper's remark decided him. He tossed the meat to old Patrick and turned away. No one should see how his mouth watered for the forbidden flesh.

On the next day, the other prisoners were served with scraps of beef, peas and rice, but the keeper again gave Joel pork, saying: "Provost's orders for his favorite." Joel knocked the meat out of his hand, and was cuffed in return.

Perhaps it was foolish to starve for rules laid down thousands of years ago. Indeed, since coming to the Colonies, Joel had not been rigid about eating only *kosher* food. But this was a deliberate challenge; it was a test of his faith and his Jewish pride. He swore that if he died for it, he would not touch the Provost's pork.

"Is it a saint you're trying to be?" asked Patrick. "When you get to Heaven, put in a word for us sinners here below."

After some days, too weak to stand, Joel crawled to a corner and lay there. He had always enjoyed eating, and now

31

all he could think of was food: golden roasted chickens and dumplings swimming in gravy; nuts and raisins and wine for the harvest festival; the stuffed fish his mother had used to make for the Sabbath. Each day when the jailer set the pork by his side, Joel turned his face to the wall.

One night he roused from stupor thinking he saw a vision. The food piled on a wooden trencher was not succulent and savory like his mother's cookery, but it was food. Patrick's red-rimmed, watery eyes were watching him, not with malice but with pity and admiration. " 'Tis a bit of ours we hid for you. Eat, lad—there be not a piece of pig in the lot."

The platter swam before Joel's eyes. Dizzily he reminded himself that this meat too, taken from beasts that had not been slaughtered according to ritual, was against the teachings of the Law. For a moment he struggled weakly to refuse it, even when Patrick held a piece up to his lips. But the sight of it, the odor of the greasy stew, was too much for his overpowering hunger. He did not wait to thank, but stuffed it down like a wolf. Because of his greedy haste, he was violently ill soon after.

The next night, when the jailer had gone, the others brought him bits of their dinner again. Surely the Lord would not want him to die in order to prove further that he was a believing Jew. He would do better, Joel thought, to live and work for more important principles of his faith. The Provost and the jailer, in their ignorance, knew only that pork was forbidden, and this Joel, as a gesture of defiance, continued to turn down. And after a while, seeing that the Jew had neither given in, nor, miraculously, died of his stub-

32

bornness, the Provost grew tired of this special baiting, and turned to thinking up more general tortures.

It was June by now, and the jail lay baking in the sun, its stone walls acting like an oven. Even when the wind from the sea cooled the citizens of Boston, no breeze ever penetrated the small windows of the cells. The inmates moaned that they were suffocating, and the jailer told them that the Provost was sick of their cries, but to show how kind and merciful he was, he had ordered the cell doors to be opened so that they might get air and exercise in the courtyard. Day after sweltering day they waited for this promise to be kept. At last, on a morning of cold winds and lashing rain, the jailer came with a great rattling of keys, to unlock the cell doors. The unhappy prisoners shivered and shrank back. Only Joel, desperate at his own uncleanness, walked up and down the narrow courtyard in the rain, and afterward, soggy and miserable in his wet clothes, he shook as if with the ague. How corrupting was power, he thought, as his teeth chattered, whether in the hands of a king, or the king's henchmen, like the Provost. Even the most ignorant of the prisoners knew more of human kindness.

One morning Joel was awakened by the sound of a dull distant thudding, and lay waiting for the first drops to fall, longing for the cold, clean touch of the rain on his sweating flesh. Even the straw pallet felt hot under him; the beam of morning sun streaming through the window seemed to scorch the stones. The patch of sky was cloudless and blue. It was not thunder but cannon which rattled the iron doors of the cells. When the jailer came with the food ration, Joel asked him what the cannonading meant. The answer was an order

33

to mind his own business if he didn't want to get a beating. All afternoon the big guns sounded, and the sharp crackle of musketry. The acrid smell of smoke drifted in through the window; though the prisoners could not know it, Charlestown, across the river, was on fire. Joel paced the floor with the sweat pouring from him, berating his companions who had been imprisoned too long to be interested even in something which might mean their own release. Bitterly impatient, he could not discover what was happening.

Several days later, a new prisoner was thrust into the cell, and fell staggering to his knees, a frail-looking youngster with a beardless, childish face, and his arm done up in a filthy, blood-soaked rag. Joel recognized him at once as the boy he had seen in New London, volunteering to join the company of soldiers under Nathan Hale. He had often thought of this boy Abner and his sister. He did not know why young Abigail's face came to his mind so often, that ardent and impudent face with the white-blond curls framing it and the snub nose wrinkled in disgust at all Tory-lovers. The boy was very like her, but now his face was drawn with weariness and pain. Joel asked him if he suffered much from his wound.

"It's pretty sore," the boy said, "but I reckon no more than is natural."

Joel knew that the arm needed attention. He unbound it and bathed it in the day's drinking water, contributed by his cellmates. It was not a severe wound, but the bullet still remained buried in the flesh. Joel did not have instruments with which to probe nor knowledge of how to do it. He bound the arm up again with a neckerchief, and the boy thanked him, saying it felt better. Joel asked him for news of the battle.

34

"At first we were beating the tar out of the Lobsters," Abner said. "The night before, Putnam and us Connecticut Militia had dug in on Breed's Hill in Charlestown. Put said if we could mount cannon there, we could sweep all Boston with 'em, and the King's ships in the river too. About dawn they discovered us though, and the ships started throwing things. Didn't do much harm, but then the whole British Army landed and started marching up the hill like they were on parade, red coats, white britches, brass buttons and flags flying. Old Put told us to stick behind the redoubt and hold our fire till they were close. Then we let 'em have it." He shuddered. "It was a bloody shambles."

"They ran away?" Joel asked.

"They came back," Abner answered. "They ran, but the General ordered them back, and they came to be killed, obedient as hound dogs. There were just too many for us, when they kept coming. We had no powder and ball left in our horns; our fire went out like an old candle flame. Then they took me prisoner."

"What was the outcome of the battle?" Joel cried.

"The British claim a victory, but it wasn't one. They lost too many men, and they're real afraid of us now. Old Put and the Connecticut Militia will take Boston yet. They'll spring us out of jail," Abner said, sticking his chin up. "You just wait and see."

Joel felt that he had already waited a long weary while. The jail was crowded with other prisoners from Charlestown, many of them wounded, and the crowding was soon further increased by patriots of Boston, imprisoned for talking treason, spying and the like. One fellow was there only because

35

he had cheered too loudly when the Colonials shot down the British at Bunker Hill; another was jailed for talking back to a British officer. Heated political discussions now helped to pass the time. Joel was always asking questions, looking into reasons and pulling arguments apart.

"Why must you quibble so?" Abner asked irritably, for the pain of his wound left him little patience. "We wish to rule ourselves. All kings are tyrants; King George is one of the worst of them. Even my sister, who is only a girl, knows that's reason enough to rebel."

"Asking questions is my way of learning," Joel explained. "This was how we discussed the fine points of philosophy, where I was in school in Poland. I know it seems overcautious to you, but I can't help it. I think I begin to be a patriot," he said, "but if I am to fight, I must be *sure* why I do it."

But he had stored up so much anger these past months it was hard to remain calm and judicial; to remind himself that England was a country where the rights of the people had been more highly regarded than in any other part of Europe, and that Englishmen were no more a race of cruel beasts like the Provost than were his own people, the Jews. It was the present government, King George and his councilors, who were at fault.

"Tell me," he went on, "if you break from the Crown, will there be justice here, courts of law for rich and poor alike? Or will creatures like old Patrick still be thrown into jail and kept there, they do not know why?"

"My father says things are bound to be better if we win," Abner said, "because of the kind of people we Colonials are. Most of our ancestors came here in the first place looking for freedom—religious freedom and other kinds—and many of them had been in jail themselves for speaking their minds. We're bound to see that justice is done."

On other days the talk would be more personal. Abner questioned Joel about the things which made the older lad seem different from others: the manner in which he prayed, and why, on days when pork was the only food, he still abstained from eating. He told Joel of his own family, of his father and mother, his sister and his younger brother Gurdon, and of their home in Fairfield, a Connecticut town which was some twenty-five miles from New Haven, where Joel's sister and her husband lived.

"My sister Abby's a wonder," Abner said. "She's always sure of what it's right to do. She was the one made me see that we had to fight for freedom. And we'll win, too," he added, "even though we haven't as much training as the Regulars, because we're fighting for something we believe in."

"That's right," one of the Bostoners chimed in. "The King's soldiers have no will for this war—why should they? They're treated like dogs. Many times I've seen 'em lined up on the Common and shot for trying to desert. And others flogged—sometimes to death—for nothing worse than speaking saucy to an officer."

Time passed for the prisoners in sleeping, eating and talking, drearily enough. The oven of June was followed by the furnace of July; August was the very jaws of the underworld, and even in September there was no relief. Brutalities increased as the Provost grew more ill-humored, feeling the heat himself, even in his many-windowed chamber. Poor prisoners who could not pay their fines for some petty offense

37

were beaten and thrown into the dungeon, or made to stay on their knees on the stone cobbles of the yard for hours crying, "God Save the King."

"Would you still argue fine points?" Abner asked Joel.

"I lose my taste for it," Joel said, holding his ears against the cries of some poor fellow.

There was no way to escape the sounds echoing through corridor and yard: blasphemy and abuse from the prison guards, groans and cries of those in pain. Dr. Brown, a patriot surgeon who was imprisoned, went to the Provost to ask for medicines, dressing and food for the wounded. "Let them eat the heads of the nails and gnaw the planks if they are hungry," the Provost told him.

There was not much the prisoners could do to help, but even rascals like Patrick were wonderfully kind and gentle with the sufferers. By the middle of September, all but twelve of the twenty-nine taken at Charlestown had died.

Abner too was sickening with a fever, and his arm was swollen to twice its size. He lay on his pallet, shivering and burning by turns, and half out of his head. The others gave him their share of water to drink, and Joel tried to cheer him, saying that he was better, that "Old Put" and the Connecticut boys were on their way to set him free.

"Is there nothing you can do?" Joel said to the surgeon, raging at his own helplessness.

"Without instruments or medications, nothing," Dr. Brown replied. "It grieves me to say this, lad, for I know you two are friends—but there is little hope for the boy."

The end came at dawn one morning. Joel, unable to sleep, was sitting by Abner's side, watching the sick boy toss and

38

turn. Abner's fair hair was dark with sweat, his face flushed and his eyes open but unseeing. He fancied he was talking to his sister; he seemed to be defending himself. "You see, Abby," he said, "I joined up like you said I should, didn't I? Maybe I *didn't* want to go at first. But you said *you'd* go, if you were a man, and I knew you were right."

A heartless little girl this Abigail must be, Joel thought, putting his hand to Abner's. The boy clutched it and held on, as if without it he might slip away into the darkness.

"Captain Hale said I was a good soldier," he said, sounding in his weakness like a small child. His voice trailed away, repeating, "A good soldier, a good soldier . . ."

"Hush, young one," Joel said, wiping the boy's brow with a bit of dampened cloth, "your sister will know you are a good soldier—none braver."

Abner looked up at him, with eyes that were fever bright, but suddenly conscious and aware of what he was saying. "Tell her for me, Joel—promise me that you will go to Fairfield and tell Abigail that I did not run at Breed's Hill—I was afraid, but I didn't run away."

"I will tell her," Joel said.

"I am not afraid now," Abner said, closing his eyes with a sigh. Joel looked away, fighting the tears. When he looked again, the boy was dead.

He got to his feet and stood with his back to the still, pitifully frail body. Around him the other prisoners were huddled, still snoring. He thought of his childhood in Poland. This was not the first death Joel had seen. And had not his father and the boy Abner died for the same reason—because of their resistance to tyranny?

39

Though Abner was a Gentile, Joel had come to think of him in these months as a beloved younger brother. He bowed his head and softly chanted the mourner's Kaddish: " 'Yisborach v'yish-tabbach, v'yis-poar, v'yis-romam. . . . Exalted and hallowed be the name of God throughout the world. May His Kingdom come, His will be done."

He lifted his eyes to the small pale square of window, high on the dark wall. A beam of early morning sun touched the iron bars with gold.

Now he knew that he *must* fight, against such cruelty as he had seen here, and for a world where useless, unnecessary deaths would no longer be tolerated.

4.

1776

IT WAS another six months
before the besieging Colonial Army forced the British out
of Boston. When Sir William Howe and his eight thousand
troops had sailed away to Halifax, Joel and the other prisoners were set free. He was very weak, for the diet had been
close to starvation in the last months of the siege, and the
chill of the prison winter ached in his bones. Excitement carried him out through the jail-house gate although his limbs
were shaking.

Boston was a city of churches and meeting houses, and now,
from every steeple, the bells of Boston were ringing. Families and lovers that had been parted, walked with arms
around one another, unaware of the raw March wind which
made whirlpools of rubbish in the filthy streets, and the gulls
screaming and fighting over garbage heaps. The British had
left the city in a pretty mess.

The wind was cold, and Joel quickly tired of wandering.

He inquired where the Connecticut Militia could be found, made his way to the encampment, and asked to be taken to Captain Hale.

Nathan Hale had been joking with his ensign; he still looked like a boy himself, with his pink cheeks and clear blue eyes, in spite of the Captain's epaulets. Joel told of his imprisonment, and of how often, in his cell, he had thought of Hale's speech at New London. "Then I disagreed with you, sir, but now I think scholars come to where they must act. I wish to join up for a soldier."

Nathan Hale looked pityingly at the gaunt, hollow-eyed young man with the flaming hair, and skin which was the color of a corpse. "We need soldiers," he said, "but you must get your strength first."

Joel threw back his bony shoulders and passed a hand over his fuzz of red beard. "If I could be shaved and clean, you would see I look strong enough," he said. "My anger is very strong."

"Anger is not enough," Nathan Hale said. "Many join us because they are angry; when they calm down they leave us again. In this war a good soldier must be sure, as my friend Benjamin Tallmadge wrote me, that he wishes to defend 'the honor of God, a glorious country, and a happy constitution.' Defend it even when things are going badly for us."

"What sort of country and what sort of constitution will be here is not plain yet to me," Joel said. "Isn't it enough to know one fights against tyranny?"

"If you're to stick with us, you'd better know what you're fighting for, as well as what you're fighting against." Nathan Hale said. "Do you have a family in this country?"

In New Haven, Joel told him.

"Go there then," Hale said. "Tell them to pamper you and give you at least three square meals a day. Weak as you are now, you would be only a burden to the Army. This war is just beginning; there will be plenty of time to join up later."

"It means very much for me to be in your company, Captain, because—because you understand what war means," Joel said. "Give me the chance now; you will see"—a spasm of coughing kept him from going on.

Nathan Hale waited till the coughing spell was over and then he said kindly, "Don't take this as a rebuff. You need not be idle while you're regaining your strength; you can speak for our cause to all you meet. We need words as well as deeds." He took a pamphlet from his pocket. "Study this; it will give you good arguments. All the Army is reading it." He pressed coach fare on Joel, saying with a smile, "You see, I know you will repay this debt."

Joel walked away with bent head, and in his absorption, stumbled against a tall militia man who cursed him drunkenly. Joel muttered an apology, and then stiffened as he saw that it was the man Alf, the one who had been leader of the gang which had beaten up the old Tory in New London. Without recognition, the fellow went weaving blindly down the street, and Joel shrugged. One couldn't expect every man in this army to be a noble character just because he was on the patriot side.

So Joel returned to his sister Miriam, who cried out at the way he looked, scolded him briskly for it, and put him to bed as if he were a child like her own little Zipporah. The bed was soft, the linen sheets cool and unbelievably clean after a straw pallet, and when Joel at last lay down he could not rise again. Suddenly the will to struggle left him, and he lay in a stupor, sleeping feverishly. The dogwood came to bloom in a white mist along the lanes, but Joel did not see it, nor know the scent of the lilacs in the yard. It was almost summer before the fever left him.

His brother-in-law, Jacob, was a little man with a boy's sweet face and the wise patience of a patriarch. When he saw that Joel now was wakeful and fretting, he moved the bed close beside the window, so that the invalid could look down across the feathery treetops to the new-washed blue of the harbor and the red rock cliffs. It was a pleasanter view than the four walls of his room, but it did not soothe Joel as it had used to. He slept little and woke each morning in the half light to hear the birds cheeping, and later, their hymn to the rising sun. He lay idly watching the family of robins that had nested in the apple tree below the window, and the fat yellow warblers darting in and out among the green leaves. Little Zipporah, his niece, came each morning to prattle of all the new things she saw. She brought him bright pebbles and shells from the shore, a bunch of violets limp in her small eager hand, or, when her mother would trust her to carry it, a dish of strawberries still smelling of the sun. Joel thanked her solemnly, and urged her to do the eating instead of him. Only with the child Zipporah did he manage to rouse himself somewhat from his lethargy, to tell her Bible stories: about good people who were rewarded, and bad people who were punished.

"Uncle Yosele, why are you so yellow and thin?" she asked one day. "Is it because you've been wicked?"

He twisted her dark curls around his fingers, kissed her round serious face, and said, "Maybe that is what ails me, little one—it is wicked to lie here with no will for anything."

Nathan Hale was right; anger was not enough. The nightmare of Boston jail was vivid as ever, sleeping or waking; but Joel remembered that he had been angry at the Sons of Liberty too, when they had tortured the old Tory. You could not judge a cause by the number of cruel people on either side. Nathan Hale was right; you had to know what you were fighting for—as well as against.

Jacob had piled Joel's books within reach, but he had no will for studying Talmud. On top lay the pamphlet called "Common Sense" which Nathan Hale had given him. He picked it up and flipped the pages idly till a phrase caught his attention; then his candle burned all night as he read.

"Near three thousand years passed away from the creation till the Jews requested a king," Thomas Paine had written. "Till then their form of government was a kind of republic administered by a judge and the elders of the tribes." Obviously the author had studied his history in the Old Testament. Monarchy, according to the Scriptures (and Tom Paine), was a sin.

Joel read on. "Oh! Ye that love mankind! Ye that dare oppose not only the tyranny but the tyrant, Stand forth! Every spot of the Old World is over-run with oppression! Freedom hath been hunted round the Globe. Asia and Africa have long expelled her! Europe regards her like a stranger, and England hath given her warning to depart. Oh! Receive

the fugitive and prepare in time an asylum for mankind."
Joel's eyes burned with reading; he closed them and let the
pamphlet drop on the counterpane. He woke next morning
feeling for the first time that he was on the mend. He tot-
tered downstairs, and when Miriam ordered him back to bed,
threatening with her stirring spoon, he declared that he was
through with being an invalid.

He was more restless than ever now, though his knees still
buckled under him when he walked. To pacify him, Jacob
found a gentle old horse which Joel named Barnabas—"son
of exhortation"—as he jogged about the countryside doing
errands; filling his saddlebags with donations of pewter and
lead sash weights to be melted down into bullets. "Whenever
General Washington is wanting something—bullets or food
or money, maybe," Jacob told Joel, "he says, 'See what
Brother Jonathan will do.' And Governor Trumbull of
course asks us, the merchants, to help him collect whatever
it is he needs."

Often Joel intended to go to Fairfield to bring Abner
Bailie's last message to his family, but there never seemed to
be time to ride the long miles there and back. Finally he
wrote a letter, telling as gently as he could, what had happened, and promising that some day he would come in per-
son to tell them more.

One afternoon, as he approached a village on the outskirts
of New Haven, he heard drums rolling and saw the militia
drawn up on the Green. He jumped from his horse and
joined the crowd that had gathered.

On the steps of the meeting house, a selectman was reading
out an announcement. The Continental Congress had pro-

46

claimed the independence of the colonies. Thus ran the Declaration. . . .

Do they really mean this, Joel thought, filled with excitement as he listened to the words: "that all men are created equal, that they are endowed by their Creator with certain unalienable rights, that among these are life, liberty and the pursuit of happiness. . . ."

If this is truly meant, then, not because of anger, but because of faith in the future, this *is* my country, Joel thought.

"I must go to New York to join the Army," he told Jacob and Miriam.

"Like a marsh heron you are—still so thin," Miriam said as she set before him the steaming bowl of thick lentil soup which he was too excited to eat. "Why must it be New York for you? The home militia you can join here in New Haven, and still I could look after you. Why not, Yosele?"

"I must pay back the coach fare to Captain Hale," Joel said, "and keep my promise to join up with him. They tell me the Connecticut Seventh Regiment, in which he is captain, is at New York. So I must go there."

Jacob begged him to delay a little longer; there was so much to do here to supply the Army, especially if an attack on New York was coming soon, as rumor had it. "Can soldiers fight without bullets, march without food?" he asked. "I need you, Joel, to help me with these shipments." Joel reluctantly agreed to wait.

Till the middle of August he remained in New Haven. But one day he said peevishly to Miriam, "I do not need to be fattened like a pig for the slaughter. Jacob will have to do his business here without me now."

47

Jacob, this time, asked only that on reaching the city, Joel go first to see Simon Levino, a merchant with whom he had been in correspondence, to discover why he had not replied to recent letters.

Joel found Levino in his warehouse on Water Street, a portly gentleman, elegantly dressed in a black brocaded coat of the English style. He read Jacob's letter with a worried frown. "Your brother-in-law is more sanguine of the outcome than I am. He does not have the British fleet on his very doorstep—a hundred and thirty vessels in the Narrows between Staten Island and here—thirty thousand troops ready to pounce!" He got up and went to the window overlooking the East River. "Only yesterday, I am informed, a large detachment of them landed at Gravesend Bay on Long Island. Look at the smoke going up over there! Waste—sheer waste! It is the so-called Patriots burning their haystacks to keep the fodder out of the hands of the King's men."

He began to pace the floor; the boards creaked under his heavy, nervous tread. "For six days we have been expecting Howe to launch his attack—any day, any hour! And Jacob Peretz writes cheerfully that he can ship a few kegs of powder for our defense! A few kegs of powder—it will take more than that!" His jowls shook, whether from indignation or fear Joel could not tell.

"But surely," Joel said, "our Army which took Boston, can also keep this city from the English?"

Levino shrugged. "It is a raggle-taggle army, untrained and unruly, drunk and disorderly." He sighed, stopped his pacing, looked at Joel as if noticing him for the first time, and said more kindly, "Will you stay the night with us, young

48

man? I would not like to see you spend this Sabbath eve alone among strangers."

Joel thanked him and said he would be pleased.

"I shall tell my good wife to expect you before sundown," Levino said.

Joel picked up his portmanteau; in the meantime he would see something of the city. At first it did not seem much changed from the day of his first arrival a year and a half before. Only that the business of its crowded streets seemed suspended, waiting. Outside Levino's warehouse, idle ships nudged one another side by side with their bowsprits overhanging the cobbles and their rigging a tangled web against the sky. There were more cannons than merchandise upon the wharves, and the narrow avenues between the step-roofed Dutch houses were torn with excavations. Often Joel had to double back to avoid a barricade or an entrenchment.

A battery of guns faced the East River from the foot of a cemetery; the inscriptions on the graves were in Hebrew. Joel sat down on a stone and mopped his forehead. The August heat was so heavy that the whole city seemed to lie breathless beneath it, waiting for the attack. Around the graves, the grass was trampled and worn, and the inscriptions were very old. Spanish names, mostly, and foreign places of birth. It was strange, and yet fitting, Joel thought, as he rose to wander on, that the warlike defenses of liberty should be planted among the peaceful Jewish dead who, on these shores, had first found refuge from persecution.

There were many soldiers in the streets, some in uniform and some in Yankee homespun with feathers in their hats. Joel asked one if he knew where the Seventh Connecticut was

49

encamped. "Up near Harlem, I reckon," the man said. "A good ways out o'town, on the way to King's Bridge." It was too late today to hunt for Captain Hale so far afield. Joel thanked the soldier and turned his steps toward the address Levino had given him.

A maidservant ushered him into a low-ceilinged, white paneled parlor where the mistress of the house rose to greet him, pale and slender, with the white hands and jet-black hair of a Spanish lady. Her silken skirts were so wide they almost hid her two daughters seated behind her: a thin alert child of eleven and a young woman of great beauty.

In the dining room, the table was set with a fine white cloth, with the wine in a silver cup and the fresh-baked Sabbath loaf in a silver basket. The lighting of the candles and the blessing were not very different from the Sabbath celebrations Joel knew, but he was awkward and shy, unused to such rich surroundings: the gleaming mahogany furniture, the silver service, the women in silken gowns and jeweled earrings. When they had eaten, and had returned to the parlor, Rachel, the older daughter, turned her brilliant dark eyes upon him and said, "Where have you been spending your time since coming to this country, sir? My father tells me you are Polish-born." It was as if she had said, how did her father dare to entertain such a barbarian?

"In Connecticut—and Boston," Joel said.

She looked at him with new interest. "Boston? They say it was very gay there before the British left."

"I did not so find it," Joel said shortly. The conversation was interrupted by a young man in the uniform of a Continental lieutenant who bounded into the room and was introduced to Joel as the son of the house. He crossed the floor in long strides and kissed his mother's hand. She embraced him. "When you did not come by sundown, David," she said, "we feared your Sabbath leave had not been granted."

"Fort Washington is a long ride from here, Mamma," he answered. Between them there passed a look of special affection and understanding. The two almost identical aquiline profiles were Roman faces from an antique coin.

David drew his younger sister Judith into a corner and whispered something. "No one thinks so but you," she said, putting her hands up to hide her blushes. Joel guessed that her brother had complimented her on her looks, although actually she was rather plain, save for the wide-set, violet eyes.

"And how is the belle of New York tonight?" David asked Rachel.

"Your sister finds it dull," said Mistress Levino. For Joel's benefit she added, "My older daughter spent a season in London, with our relatives there, and New York seems like a country village to her now. This is unfortunate, at least David and I think so." She smiled across the room at Rachel. "Although it *is* dull for a young woman when all the young men have joined the Army."

Rachel looked sullen and did not answer. In the awkward silence that followed, a rattle of musketry came faintly through the windows, thrown wide to catch the breeze off the river.

Simon Levino started.

"Skirmishing among the outposts in Flatbush," David commented. "What a relief it would be to have the action begin!"

Rachel moved impatiently. "How long are *you* going to stick to your foolish notions, brother?" she said. "Everyone knows that New York will surrender, and that will be the end of your Revolution. Do you look forward to being a prisoner of war?"

"Your sister is right, David," Levino said.

"There are worse things than being a prisoner of war," his son replied.

From across the street there came the crash of a breaking window pane, a voice raised in protest, soon drowned out by curses and laughter. Someone pounded loudly on the door of the Levino house.

Simon Levino shuddered. "The Sons of Liberty—Tory-riding again. Surely they do not think I am a Tory . . ."

"I will take care of them," David said, going to the door, where the sight of his Continental uniform silenced the crowd. He spoke a few low words, closed the door and came back to the parlor. The noises receded down the street.

"There you have the trouble," Levino said. "As you know, my son, I went along with Mr. Livingston and other respectable Whigs while there was some chance that a display of strength would make the King see the unwisdom of measures which restrict our trade. But I cannot make a party with radicals—those that are taking over now. The behavior of the Sons of Liberty is scandalous. They are well called 'the Sons of License'!"

"Not all of them, Papa. The Sons of Liberty have done brave work for the cause. And you would not call our leaders radicals, would you?" David asked. "Such men as Samuel Adams, John Hancock and Thomas Jefferson? Or the Continental Congress itself?"

"Congress!" the elder Levino sputtered. "A mob of petti-fogging lawyers! We old Jewish families should remember the allegiance we owe to the Crown. After all, under Peter Stuyvesant, and the Dutch, we did not fare so well; we should be grateful that since New York has been English, we have received our rights."

"You are grateful for small privileges, my father," David said scornfully. "We are still second class citizens—although I grant, so are many Gentiles. One must have money, prop-erty, *and* acknowledge the Christian faith to be a proper Colonial citizen. Do you remember what Tom Paine said?"

"I would not allow the words of that rabble-rouser in my house!" the merchant said.

"I have read it," Joel said.

David turned to him, his face alight. "Do you recall the passage—that we could raise here 'an asylum for mankind'?"

"I remember well," Joel said.

Simon Levino stepped between the two young men, half pleading, half scornful. "The words sound noble—but the author is deluding you! 'An asylum for mankind'—well, yes, in the far distant future, perhaps. Now we must be practical. We Jews *cannot* afford to be called radicals. They always accuse us of it."

"When they don't say we care only for moneybags," Joel said. "What we can't afford is to pay attention to such things."

"Bravo!" cried David.

"You have come to this country too recently perhaps to un-derstand the situation," Levino said to Joel.

"I understand," Joel said, forgetting his manners. "Better than you who don't know the inside of a British jail."

53

Rachel looked accusingly at her father. "I did not expect you to bring home a jailbird, Papa!"

Joel stood up and bowed. "I go now. But first I will tell you I was falsely accused, had no trial, and was unjustly treated. So with many others. It was enough to make me turn against the government that allows such things."

David put a hand on his arm. "It is my sister who does not understand. Do not go, for you and I have a lot to talk about."

And Simon Levino, looking with worried eyes from one of his children to the other, said, "These are troublesome times, when even one's own family is split apart. Our whole congregation is torn with differences."

"If you would listen to Gershom Seixas, Papa," David said, "you might be more convinced than by my arguments."

"The *Hazan* meddles in things that are not his business," said Levino angrily. "Did we choose him to preach to us of politics?"

Mistress Levino rose with a rustling of her silken skirts. "These are times when we should all have faith in one another, no matter how we differ." She turned to Joel, smiling. "I must ask your forgiveness for my daughter's rudeness. Say that you will remain here, and go with us to the Synagogue on the Sabbath morn. Then you can judge of Rabbi Seixas for yourself."

It would be good to hear services in a real house of worship; not since Warsaw had Joel been in a Jewish community large enough to afford one. Also he was curious to see this rabbi who meddled in politics. He bowed and said, "If you truly wish it, I will be glad to stay."

54

5.

MORNING air had no freshness but lay hot and stagnant in the crooked narrow lanes as Joel walked to the Synagogue with Simon Levino and his son David. The gutters of Mill Street steamed and above them tiny insects did a dizzy dance. Inside the stone hall it was cooler at first, but soon so many members of the congregation were crowding the benches that it was almost hot enough to melt the candles in the tall brass candlesticks before the Ark and in the chandeliers hanging from the balcony where the women sat.

The men were solid citizens, dressed in sober but rich dark clothes. Young men were few, and with most of these, as with David, the striped silk prayer shawls were draped over Continental uniforms. Before services began, there was much whispering and consultation among the elders, and an atmosphere of strain not in keeping with the Sabbath.

Even the young rabbi, dignified in his robes, seemed to be struggling for serenity. As he held up the scrolls of the Law to the congregation, there was special intensity in his voice. Joel was soon lost in an upsurge of feeling as he joined in chanting the old Hebrew responses he had known since childhood.

When the scrolls had been returned to the Ark, Gershom Seixas mounted the platform. The hall was filled with the sound of anxious waiting: heavy breathing, a nervous cough, the rustle of garments, the shuffle of a foot against the floor.

"Not very long ago in this same place," Gershom Seixas said in English, "I prayed that the heart of King George and the hearts of his councilors might be moved to turn away their fierce wrath from our North America. I prayed that there might be no more blood shed in these countries and that God might plant an everlasting peace between Great Britain and her colonies. But it was not to be."

He took a text from Exodus and spoke of liberty, how it had been a dear thing to the Jews ever since the Children of Israel were freed from bondage in Egypt. He spoke of the periods of history and the many lands where they had fought for it.

He bowed his head for a moment, then lifted his face and said, in a low voice, "Today may be the last time we worship in this, our beloved Synagogue. The enemy is at our gates. His cause is not a just cause."

Again he searched the faces around him, row on row. "I have discussed this with you," he said. "Most of you believe, as I do, that from this day the doors of our house of worship should be closed. For if we continue after the enemy comes,

56

we give sanction to tyranny. We must go, and seek our freedom elsewhere, trusting that right will prevail and that some day we may meet here again."

There were tears in the eyes of the congregation; even the Tories among them wept.

At the close of the services, David Levino clasped Joel's hand, saying, "*Shabbat Shalom*—a peaceful Sabbath to you." Both young men were conscious of the irony of the words, with the British priming their guns just across the river.

Outside the hall, where friends usually stopped to wish each other a good Sabbath, a great argument began.

"But of course the *Hazan* was right," said one. "If we do not stand up for freedom, who will?"

"He was entirely wrong," said another. "The law of the King is the law of the land. Freedom of worship is all that concerns us—and don't we have that here?"

"Yes, but—" said the first man, when a third interrupted with the news that Gershom Seixas intended to pack up the scrolls and prayer books, all the sacred objects, and take them away from the city so that they might not fall into Tory hands. The argument waxed hotter; and many families hurried home to discuss in private whether *they* should remain in New York or seek refuge with Patriots elsewhere, in Norwalk, Stratford and Philadelphia. One thing was sure: no one thought the city could be held.

"Even General Washington doesn't think so."

"Why then does he try?"

"Because the Congress has ordered it."

David, his Sabbath leave over, was saying good-by to his family, in haste to rejoin the garrison of the fort, named for

General Washington, which had recently been built at the upper end of Manhattan.

"I will go with you," Joel said.

"It is no place for an untrained recruit, my friend," David said. "And you are needed here—to fight from street to street and house to house, if necessary."

"It is true I don't know one end of a musket from another," Joel said, smiling. "While for street fighting I had some training already in Poland."

"Stay with my family, I beg of you," David said. "In the next few days we'll know better where and how to use new troops. Right now there's too much else to think about."

So once more Joel could not keep his promise to return to Nathan Hale. Instead he joined those who were practicing how they could defend the city, marching and drilling with a few ancient firearms. He came back to the Levino household each night with mixed feelings, as the feelings of the family itself were mixed. Simon Levino would not hear of plans to leave the city; there was no reason why he should not be comfortable under the British if they came. Mistress Levino was gracious and kind, but distracted, disapproving her husband's viewpoint, and too dutiful a wife to say so. Judith, when she forgot her shyness, was as much a rebel as her brother David.

"Mr. Salomon, the only Polish gentleman we knew till you came, had to leave Poland because of a Revolution there too," she said. "He doesn't visit us anymore; Papa doesn't approve of him. He says Mr. Salomon has too many dealings with the Sons of Liberty."

Rachel, after the first evening, turned her charm in Joel's direction. He felt it was only because no other young men were available at the time, having no idea that his face was good to look upon, and that she sensed in him, under the controlled manner, an inner fierceness which she found intriguing. He turned her witticisms aside and did not unbend.

On Monday, messengers reported that British soldiers were on the march toward Brooklyn from their landing place at Gravesend Beach. This movement might be only a distraction, with the main attack to come elsewhere. But where, and when? On Tuesday Joel woke at dawn to cannon fire rattling the window frames. He threw on his clothes and ran from the room. At the stair landing he met Judith, looking older than her eleven years in her long white gown. "Is it the battle?" she asked. "God send victory to General Washington!"

Sunrise was sulphurous over the East River, which moved sluggishly seaward, streaked gray and crimson. Nothing could be seen of the Brooklyn shore but a red haze beyond which the cannons bayed, deep-throated and ominous. The ominous rumors grew with the daylight: the battle was going badly; Washington had crossed over to take command; the Americans had been outflanked, hundreds killed and captured.

Joel fumed, but there was no way for a civilian to get across the river, and even if there had been, he had no musket and did not know how to use one. He was disgusted with his own helplessness and with the sense that all he did, had done, for months, was wait and wait and talk about fighting.

On the water front, crowds milled about: dock loungers,

beggars, workmen glad to make this an excuse for a holiday. The taverns were doing a big business, and, as the ale flowed, the mob grew bold and began to look for Tories to torment. The Tories barred their doors and sat in their parlors praying that the British would come soon to restore law and order. Among the water-front ruffians, there were already some who were changing their tune: the King's men would win; they'd said so right along! Fist fights were breaking out all over the place.

When night fell there was no longer any sound of battle from across the river. Wednesday dawned heavily in hot damp silence; no sunrise, no cannon fire, only a warm drizzle from the saturated gray sky.

Joel scribbled a note to his hostess and slipped away. He did not know how he would get nearer to the fighting, but he knew he could no longer rest comfortably in a soft bed in Simon Levino's house.

The drizzle turned to a downpour. It was no weather for fighting with muskets, but even so the silence seemed more ill-omened than the gunfire of the day before. Perhaps Washington had surrendered, and this was the end. No one knew what was happening and not even the bold and curious could get across the river to find out. Some said that the boats swarming out there in the driving rain halfway to Long Island were ferrying across reinforcements.

It was still raining by nightfall. Joel sought shelter in the doorway of a warehouse, and, exhausted with pacing up and down, dozed fitfully till voices on the river and the creak of oars roused him toward morning. He ran to the end of the wharf to stare out through the slanting gray curtain of rain, and saw a whaleboat drawing in slowly to the piling where a cluster of men had gathered.

"Hello-o there!" called a man in oilskins, standing at the stern. "Can any of you fellows pull an oar? We're going across the river and we're shorthanded for crew."

Joel pressed forward through the knot of men, but no one else moved or volunteered.

"It's General Washington's orders!" the seaman snapped. "What's the matter with you fellers? Are you lily livered? Afeard of being drownded?"

"Ain't no sense in going across the river now," a man growled. "It's just sending good money after bad."

"Money, money, money!" said the Yankee scornfully. "Money's God to you Yorkers, ain't it?"

"Washington had ought to know when he's licked," the man on the dock said sullenly.

Joel had made his way to the edge of the wharf by now. "Who says Washington is licked?" he cried. "We can't see what goes on over there, can we? And if the fight goes badly, it is my fault—and yours—and yours—" he pointed an accusing finger. "It is because we haven't joined up with Washington sooner." He jumped down into the boat, picked up an oar and shook it at those on the dock. "The captain's not even asking us to shoot. He's only asking that we row. Lily-livers—he is right!"

"Mulish dolts, that's what you are," the skipper added.

The group on the dock growled and grumbled, some of them threateningly. A burly, bearded Dutchman lumbered over and lowered himself into the whaleboat. "Come on, fellas—let's show the outlanders they're not so smart."

With shamed faces, the dock loungers scrambled aboard to fill the rowers' benches.

"That's better," said the captain. "Let's see if we can't walk away handsome now!"

When they had fended off from the wharf, he told his crew briefly that he was one of Colonel Glover's regiment of Marblehead fishermen which had orders to bring every boat they could find to Long Island to ferry back the sick and wounded. "Out in the stream there's British ships about. Keep your mouths shut, all of you fellows, and see if you can't row without catching any crabs."

6.

BY THE time they reached
the Long Island shore, boats were crowding in, whaleboats,
sailing boats, fishing craft—anything that would stay afloat,
gathered from all the rivers that bounded Manhattan Island,
and from the lower Sound as well. Glover's men, in oilskins
or blue jackets, were bossing the beaching of them and strip-
ping them of everything that took up unnecessary room:
extra anchors and sails, lobster pots, nets and tackle. Behind
the gray curtain of falling rain there was only the strange
silence; on the trampled, muddy shore a mounted officer was
consulting with Colonel Glover.

"We'll be ready to start ferrying by evening, Lieutenant,"
Glover said. "You can tell the General that."

The officer saluted, spurred his horse, and vanished into
the rain.

"Who is the lieutenant?" Joel asked, intrigued by the
young officer's sensitive, intelligent face.

"Ben Tallmadge—a smart soldier for all his book learning," the fisherman said.

So this must be the schoolmaster of Wethersfield, Nathan Hale's friend. Joel wondered where Captain Hale himself might be.

It was hot work hauling the heavy boat gear. Joel stripped off his shirt and stopped now and then to wring the rain from his sodden breeches.

"I can see your ribs, boy," said the fisherman whom he was helping. "Had the distemper lately?"

Joel straightened his back and flexed his tired muscles. "No, I was in a British prison where they did not feed us much. Thin I may be, but I am not weak—the prison showed me what I needed to know."

Dusk came early that gloomy summer evening. With the dusk, the first bedraggled survivors of the battle began to straggle down to the shore. Joel thought that he had never seen faces so bewildered and hopeless. Terror he had seen in Poland, and pain, but not this look of utter confusion. One soldier, with a bandaged head, walked in a daze straight for the river. Above the bandage, red hair sprouted.

Joel ran over and grabbed him. A grin dawned on the powder-blackened face. "Joe, you do turn up unexpected-like," Denis Leary said.

Joel led him to a seat in the boat, and Denis collapsed with his head in his hands. "I'm a lucky one to be out of this Hell," he moaned. "I knew Saint Patrick must still be watching over me when the Leftenant said our company was to be relieved."

The trickle of survivors was becoming a steady stream of men marching down to the shore. This could not be relief for the wounded only; it looked like full-scale retreat. In a panic lest they be left behind, a group suddenly broke formation to push and elbow each other out of the way; the disorder spread to a near riot. Then Joel had his first glimpse of General Washington, a tall lean man with a furious white face, lashing out with tongue and sword till discipline was restored.

It was raining harder than ever; a fierce east wind was lashing the river into foam; the tide boiled down from Hell Gate. The rain had hidden the fleeing Colonials from their enemies, but no craft could carry them to safety across the river in this. And here on the shore they were exposed to fire without woods or ditches to shelter them.

They lay huddled in the boats exhausted. A boy was sobbing; another laughed hysterically. No one cared what happened to the Revolution; all they wanted was to get away. Some cursed General Washington, saying the whole battle had been one blunder after another. If the British came upon them now, they would be slaughtered like sitting ducks.

A fisherman sniffed the wind. "Coming round to southerly and letting up a bit—but it ain't clearing yet. Leastways I hope it don't—there's too many British men-of-war out in that river could spot us of a bright starry night."

The wind blew from the ocean, bringing with it the taste of salt and the fog; at first a thin mist veiling the last stragglers on the shore and the heaps of gear discarded in the mud. Then it thickened to wrap each boat in a cloak of gray, and where there had been a line reaching in each direction as far as the eye could see, there were now so many separate worlds, knowing only by sound that other worlds existed.

"That you, Caleb?" a voice with a down-East twang asked.

"Mought be," said the skipper of Joel's boat. "I can't rightly see one end of myself from the other."

"Colonel says to shove off. Kin you find your way across this consarned river?"

"Fog ain't no news to me," the skipper said. "Get your carcasses aboard fast," he ordered the crew.

It was half an hour before midnight. As the boat pulled out, the shore spat musket fire; boots sloshed through the mud, and disappointed shouts followed them.

Denis raised his head feebly. "It's the bloodthirsty Hessians. They've been hunting us up and down like it was a pig sticking." A moment later he added, "Captain Hale says they're human, but I don't go along with him on that."

"Where is Captain Hale?" Joel panted between oar strokes.

"Last time I saw him—that was yesterday—he was standing up on the Brooklyn fortification, lookin' around as if he thought a bullet couldn't hit him. I never saw a man that did so much thinking, who thought so little o' death," Denis said.

Out on the river, the fleet of transports soon lost each other. The boat in which Joel pulled an oar moved slowly in a pool of black water blurring off into soggy velvet. Dank vapors floated across Joel's face. Oarlocks creaked, and a volunteer, unaccustomed to rowing, made a great splash. The skipper pointed into space. "Out there is a fleet of British

66

ships of the line," he whispered. "Maybe they won't see us, thanks to the pea soup, but they'll hear us if we come close and ain't careful. One broadside and we'd be cast like bread upon the waters!"

"And me, I can't no-wise swim," another fisherman said.

They dipped their oars again, even the wharf rats trying to be silent as Indian paddlers. The skipper was feeling his way across the river by keeping broadside to the current, but Joel wondered how he knew where on Manhattan they would land, or even whether it might not be in the lower harbor, drifting out to sea.

Suddenly, just over their shoulders, a ship's bell rang eight times. They backed water hastily. A wounded man groaned; another clamped a hand over his mouth. They slid by the dim glow of a riding light and heard the tide lisping against an anchor chain, but of the hull and spars of the man-of-war they could see nothing.

Like a tired water beetle, the boat crawled in to the shelter of the familiar wharves. Soon they were jostling and fending off from other boats, and the defeated army spilled out on dry land. What happened in the future they did not care, so long as they could sleep now. Maybe the Commander in Chief hadn't been so all-fired stupid after all; at least he'd saved his army, what there was left of it.

They rolled up to sleep in warehouses, or careened off down the street to bang on the doors of sleeping house-holders, and when they were denied admission by timid burghers, made the hour before dawn hideous with their curses. Was this any way to treat a soldier of Liberty? They broke into taverns and shops, and helped themselves to any-

67

thing handy before stretching out under a counter or a table.

Joel draped his wounded friend's arm around his shoulders and half-carried him from the boat. He could think of no place where Denis could find rest and care but the Levino house. He led him to the door and pounded on the polished brass knocker. There was a long wait before he heard timid footsteps creeping down the stairs, and Simon Levino's frightened voice asking what was wanted at this uncivilized hour.

"Shelter and asylum," Joel said.

When Levino saw the mud-stained Continental uniform, he cried out, "No, no! My life would not be worth a shilling if the British should discover that I harbored a Rebel soldier. Take him somewhere else."

"The British are not here yet," Joel said angrily. "Would you turn away your own son if he were wounded? He too is a Rebel soldier."

"Please God, David is safe at Fort Washington," Levino mumbled. "Go to Haym Salomon—he may take you in." Then as Joel, supporting the half-conscious Denis, turned bitterly away, he added, "Forgive me—I must think first of my daughters."

Salomon welcomed Joel without question and helped carry Denis to a bed, saying he would summon a surgeon. "Will you not also stay and rest?" he said to Joel.

"I must go to Harlem," Joel said. "What will happen to my friend if the British come here?"

"He will be safely hidden, never fear. Go in peace," Salomon said.

"*Shalom*," Joel replied. He knew, even in this brief en-

68

counter, that the frail little man understood what was at stake, and that, unlike Levino, he was not afraid.

The first sunbeams were breaking hot through the pearly mist as he tramped wearily up the Broad Way to the outskirts of the town. Beyond Greenwich Village, the lovely countryside was beginning to look autumnal; the fields were egg-yellow with goldenrod and purple-patched with asters; meadow grass was turning rosy on hills crowned by the white houses of prosperous Dutch gentry. The weeds by the road still gleamed wet with yesterday's rain, and everywhere soldiers were sleeping, lying in the ditches or curled up under hedgerows. Joel yawned and rubbed his eyes; the temptation to lie down himself was very great; he was falling asleep as he walked. He turned off the road to the tempting shade of shrubbery, pushed aside the branches and came upon two privates asleep with their muskets beside them. At the crackling twigs one opened his eyes to stare and said, "What're you after, Red? *You* ain't a soldier, be you?"

"Not yet," Joel said, and asked, did the soldier know where the Connecticut contingent had got to?

The man waved a vague hand toward the north. "Some-'eres up in Harlem. Why for?"

"To join up," Joel said.

"*Join up!*" the soldier poked his companion. "Hey, Zeke, here's a loon says he's goin' to join up *now!*"

The second soldier roused, blinked at Joel unbelievingly, and went back to snoring.

"Why not—now?" Joel asked.

"Because, man, this war's near over," the soldier said. "The Lobsters'll do a little more cleaning up and that'll be

69

the end of it. I don't figure to be cleaned up. I'm going home."

Deserting, Joel thought. He frowned, and the soldier went on belligerently. "A man has a right to go back to his wife and children to look after them, come winter. Who's going to cut the firewood, if he don't? Lor', I ain't the only one—there's thousands doing it."

"You don't care who wins?" Joel asked.

"Oh sure—if there was a chance our side would win. I'd ruther not have a king over me, but I had my bellyful of fighting at Brooklyn. I'm quitting. And if you have any sense, young fellow, you won't even start."

"Let the fire-eaters fight it out," said the other soldier. "Me too—I want to go home."

The Continental Army, Joel gathered, was spiritless and sullen. Autumn was the time of year when the men wanted to sit by their own firesides drinking cider and munching apples—not lying on the ground without tents at night and running away from Hessian savages by day. If they were licked, why not admit that they were licked and get on with the normal chores of living?

Joel rolled over on his stomach and buried his face in his arms. He was green and inexperienced, in no position to argue with men who had known battle. But this fight was his fight now, even if it was a losing one. He was late in joining —perhaps too late—but one did not walk out just because victory was uncertain; then, least of all.

70

7.

JOEL spent his first two weeks in the army sweating with pickaxe and shovel. Work was a relief, but there were other things about being a soldier that worried his conscience, he found. The labor expected of him on the Sabbath, for instance. But had not the Maccabees declared it permissible to fight in self-defense, even on the day of rest? And was not this the same sort of an emergency? From the redoubts along the East River, he could see the bivouacs of General Howe on the opposite shore stretching from the Brooklyn battleground to where the river islands would make convenient steppingstones for an invader. Only the swirling tide of Hell Gate protected Manhattan there. In the city the Tory burghers impatiently waited the British invasion so order could be restored and business resumed. In the Army, campfire talk was about where Howe would attack next; which brigades would have

71

to bear the brunt of it. The Commander in Chief had been obliged to spread his army very thin in the various danger spots, for he had few soldiers left; so many had deserted.

Nathan Hale had been transferred to a company of Rangers, and Joel had been unable to get in touch with him.

One night, with other raw recruits from Connecticut, Joel was sent to work on the trenches at Kip's Bay, a few miles above the city. It had been a long hard march to get there. The soldiers complained at having to dig more ditches, and, being independent Yankees, told their officers they'd be blessed if they'd touch a shovel till morning.

Joel lay on the ground, lulled by the lapping of the river tide and the voice of the watch. He buried his head in his arms and dozed off into a labyrinth of nightmares. Whenever, afterward, he remembered the following day, it was as if he had never awakened from those evil dreams. None of it made sense: the screaming and confusion; the officers beating on their men, begging them to get up; the monster ships of war looming through swirling morning mists out in the river. Joel struggled to his feet, still half asleep. Along the monsters' sides, open gun ports grinned like missing teeth.

Then from these caverns, the guns snaked out. Joel flung up one arm to hide his eyes, dropped his gun to clutch his ears. The world was breaking apart in the thunder and lightning of the broadsides from those mighty ships. Frantically he recovered his gun, and pointed it feebly at the curtain of smoke and flame. The curtain drifted up slowly to show a crescent of landing barges gracefully dipping oars, blossoming with scarlet coats and spiked with glittering bayonets. And the relentless broadsides boomed again, covering the landing.

Joel and his fellows stood gaping at the stony-faced ranks which came with precise rhythm and swing, up from the landing place. Tramp, tramp, tramp—one, two, three—like mechanical men the Grenadiers raised their polished weapons to their shoulders and fired. A broadside echoed the crackle of the volley; grapeshot and ball were hailing down. All around Joel, sobbing boys were throwing away their muskets and running. Some babbled like the inmates of a madhouse as they ran. This was the very stuff of madness; flashes that blinded; the pounding of cannon that deafened you and never stopped; billowing yellow fog that smelled of sulphur and gunpowder and blood.

Most of the Colonials had never been under fire before; certainly not under the fire of broadsides from ships of war. They were country boys, used to hunting squirrels and foxes; good marksmen, but undisciplined. They broke and ran, kicking aside the bodies of the fallen.

They paid no attention to the frantic orders of their officers, but there was one moment when they almost rallied. A haggard man on a hard-breathing, sweat-soaked horse galloped up, cursing and begging them to stand. They felt ashamed, but terror lashed them more fiercely. They turned their backs on their Commander in Chief and fled.

"Are these the men with whom I am to defend America?" cried Washington, and spurred alone toward the British lines, driven mad by despair. A young officer snatched the bridle rein and held the horse till the General came to his senses.

Joel was caught up with his fellows, in the madness of running. Over fields and byways, trampling down vegetable patches, through hog wallows and manure piles—anything to get away from that bloody shore. Then the fugitives scattered, each man for himself, and some of them were shot down like rabbits by grinning, grunting Hessians.

Joel lost himself in the country lanes. A sultry sun had drilled through the morning mist; no breath of wind stirred the drooping leaves, and the stubbled fields were parched yellow as desert sand. He licked his cracked lips and the salt drops that trickled down. Each step seemed more than he could take. He saw a farmer boy, lying under a tree, smiling up at the sky through the green-flecked boughs, and thought he would ask him if it was safe to rest here for a moment in the shade. At the sound of his approaching footsteps, the boy did not stir, for all that his eyes were wide. His shirt front was soaked with blood.

Beyond a bank of trees, voices came to Joel, shouting orders in a tongue he well knew and hated; the tongue that all the oppressed of Europe knew, language of the mercenaries whom every petty monarch used to fight his wars and put down rebellions. The Hessians were coming up over the hill and Joel fled in the opposite direction. He did not know that he was headed back toward the city, nor that the whole Colonial Army was in retreat again, straggling up toward Washington's headquarters in Harlem. By the time he reached the first houses on the outskirts, the streets were swarming with Redcoats; he was already cut off. Joel quickly dodged around a corner, and ran again, darting down alleys, taking shelter behind barrels and rubbish heaps. He ducked

74

and hid until dusk, but after sunset it was no better; sentries were policing the streets with flares and muskets. At last, not knowing what else to do, he sought refuge with Haym Salomon.

He lay that night at Salomon's lodging, feeling himself a deserter. What were they doing, what were they saying, at Washington's headquarters? That the Revolution was doomed, since those who were supposed to fight for it, always ran away? That the idea had just been a foolish dream? If so, Joel felt as responsible for the disaster as any. After all his brave talk, when the chance to prove himself came, had he remembered how Abner Bailie had died, or the noble, hopeful words of Tom Paine?

No, he had run away. It was no comfort that others had run too.

In the morning, both Denis and Haym Salomon tried to tell him that he was blaming himself unduly. Many had been trapped the day before. Joel, at least, had so far managed to escape capture, and he was free to fight again.

"I must get to Harlem at once," Joel said. "I will find a way somehow; this morning I will go."

"You'll go straight into enemy hands if you try it," Salomon told him. "I will arrange to sneak you through the lines as soon as it is possible; I have friends who know how to do these things. Only have patience."

"Wait with me, Joe," Denis said. "In a few days I'll be fit as a fiddle and then the two of us can travel together— it's better than trying it alone."

Joel reluctantly agreed and impatiently awaited his host's word. The Sons of Liberty had plans afoot, but what they

75

were, Haym Salomon would not say. It was tedious hiding like a weasel, sometimes crouching for hours in a hole in cellar or attic, while the soldiers of Cunningham, the British Provost, searched the house. Cunningham was suspicious of Salomon, but he had not been able to pin anything on him as yet.

One night some hours before dawn, Joel started up from bed in the room he shared with Denis, aroused by the furious ringing of alarm bells. Still half-asleep, he hoped it was the Patriots taking the city again. The window panes were lit with a red and flickering glare, and from somewhere downtown near Whitehall slip, flames were mounting over the rooftops to the spire of Trinity Church. You could hear the pounding of feet on the cobbles, the cries of housewives trying to save their precious possessions, the shouts of British soldiers who were attempting to dash water on the fire. Crouching by the window, Denis said, "It's the whole city is burning up!"

Joel grabbed his arm. "This—it is our chance! In all this excitement, who will think to ask what we are or why we run away? It is now, Denis, or maybe not ever!"

Salomon agreed that they should go. "The Provost knows the Sons of Liberty meet here in this house—and he knows they spoke of setting fire to the city. He is sure to send a searching party; maybe he even will arrest me."

"Come with us!" Joel said.

"No, that would be admitting guilt—and actually, I didn't do it; I don't know who did. If I can convince the Provost of this, I can still be useful here. So go quickly—and good luck to you both."

76

They opened the house door, looked this way and that, and slipped out. But before they had gone many paces, a voice hailed them.

"You there!" cried a Grenadier, appearing from nowhere and catching Denis by the ear. Joel tried to shrink back, but the prick of a sword dug him out of the shadows. "Why are you two carrot-topped rascals not fighting the fire like every other honest citizen?" the Britisher demanded. "Only dirty Jonathans would be skulking idly at such a time. I'll turn you over to the Provost for a pair of Rebels."

"Don't be sayin' that to a couple of King George's loyal subjects!" Denis protested. "Me brother and I were just after leaving our comfortable beds for the very purpose of helping with the fire—all we're askin' is to be showed how we can be useful."

The Grenadier stared him up and down, but neither lad wore anything that could be recognized as a uniform. And the crackling of the fire was drawing closer. A brisk wind fanning up from the harbor made the flames run like a glowing red snake from house to house. Walls roared up at its touch and roofs fell in, crashing. The Grenadier hustled Joel and Denis toward the river, where citizens had made a double line to fill leather buckets and pans and every large receptacle they had been able to find, and pass them from hand to hand. Denis and Joel were glad to join the bucket brigade; for the present they would be safe in such company.

It seemed as if nothing would ever stop the spread of the fire. Morning came, thick with a gray fog of whirling cinders. Noon went by and afternoon; Joel and Denis were still passing buckets, unable to break away.

But a shift in the wind finally stopped the march of the flames by evening, when the fire had reached an open space formed by the College Green on the West Side of the city. "Leave us find a place where we can stretch out a bit, Joe," Denis said, as the fire fighters dispersed. "If I'm shot for it, I can't move another inch this night."

So they crept behind some sacks in an abandoned shed, to nap an hour or so.

8.

IT WAS a little before dawn when Joel dragged himself from deep slumber and shook a complaining Denis out of his dreams. The streets were deserted; Yorkers and British soldiers who had been up fighting the fire for twenty-four hours were now sleeping. They took the road near the East River, for this was not so much used to reach Harlem as the wider thoroughfare to the West. And Joel knew his way in this part of the city, having worked on the redoubts and ditches here.

A smell of wet burned timbers was stale on the early morning air, and wisps of smoke still curled up lazily from the smoldering ruins downtown. But it was going to be a lovely day; the sky was clear and touched with pink where the sun would rise. The two young men walked briskly, joking about how they had got away from under the noses of the British soldiers. They covered several miles and were beginning to reach the upper part of the city where the houses

79

of the rich gentry sat on knolls overlooking the river, surrounded by their gardens and carefully kept lawns. They ducked inland to skirt the Beekman estate, now headquarters of General Howe, for here the sentries would surely be alert. And still they met no one but a few drunks wandering home from making a night of it. When they came upon a crowd gathered near a tavern, Denis was feeling bold, and his eye lit up with his usual curiosity. "It's a brawl, Joe—let's go see."

Joel held him back. "No, Denis—there are soldiers, standing at attention—something special goes on here."

"Supposing it does? None could recognize us for what we are—and they're not interested in us anyway." He shouldered his way into the crowd.

The sun was just rising; the soldiers' coats glowed like rubies and the massed cannon of the Royal Artillery parked in a field close by were brassy bright. Beyond them, towering ships of the line swung at anchor in the river. The early risers, wagoners and charwomen mostly, stood with eyes fastened on something within a hollow square formed by the company of Redcoats. Denis cried out; Joel grabbed his arm, and then he saw too. Nathan Hale was perched on a ladder under an apple tree, with a rope around his neck. He did not wear his captain's uniform but was dressed as he had been when Joel had first seen him, in the plain brown coat of a country schoolmaster. His usually pink cheeks were pale, but he stood very erect on the shaky ladder, and there was no trace of shame in his clear blue eyes. The sun touched his fair hair and the breeze of the beautiful morning lifted it gently.

At the foot of the ladder a red-faced brute of a man—Cunningham, the Provost—faced the prisoner. "This is your last chance!" Cunningham shouted. "Do you want to confess your wickedness?"

The young schoolmaster looked back at him steadily for a brief moment and for another his eyes wandered out over the heads of the crowd to the sunny fields, the sparkling river, and the clear blue sky. Then he looked at Cunningham again, and said in a ringing voice, "I only regret that I have but one life to lose for my country."

"Swing the Rebel off!" the Provost shouted.

The women in the crowd were sobbing; so was Denis. Joel was in a sweat of horror and rage, the more sickening because he was helpless. Blindly he and Denis crept from the scene of the execution, doubled a corner, broke into a run. Blindly they ran through the lanes, saying nothing, not even bothering to conceal themselves. Only once Denis muttered, "Why should I be trying so hard to save my worthless carcass when the likes of my dear Captain is gone?"

It was luck that no British patrols came upon them. Neither could tell afterward how they managed to reach Harlem, for each was deep in his own unhappy thoughts. Joel knew that he had failed in the promise he had made at Boston. He had joined up so late; he had taken to his heels like a coward at the first encounter. And now he would never be able to fight under Nathan Hale's leadership, or speak to him again.

When they reached the American lines next day, they found that the news of the hanging had already reached there.

"Spying's a dirty business," said one of the men standing by. "I wouldn't have expected a gentleman like Captain Hale to undertake it."

"If Captain Hale did it, it was no dirty business," said Denis angrily.

"It was for all of us that he did this!" Joel said, in a tight, dry voice that struggled for control. "Everything depends on knowing where the British will strike next. With more defeats, General Washington will have no army left. To shoot off a gun is little—but to go into an enemy city as a spy—that takes courage! No, it was not a dirty business, but a noble, unselfish act."

He could not get Nathan Hale's last words out of his head. He looked at the men sprawled about him in the camp, smoking their pipes, joking, complaining, like any other army. How many lives would be given before this war was over? Perhaps even his own. And how many other lives would he and his comrades take, lives of men guilty of no personal crime? One could only hope that this would be the last war for Americans, that the new country would show the world a new way of life, wanting no empire, only peace.

"The best we can do for Captain Hale, I think," Joel said, "is to fight the way he said . . . 'and never lay down our arms until we have obtained our independence!'"

White Plains; dawn of a crisp October day; the sun stretched long fingers across fields silvered with early frost. Joel nervously shifted his musket from hand to hand, looked down the barrel to see if it was clean, made sure that his

82

cartridges were at hand. He dug his toes into the ground; he would have chained himself there if he could, so that there would be no chance of his running away again. Since Kip's Bay, the others here had proved themselves. " 'Member how we whipped 'em at Harlem Heights?" said one. "Them Britishers felt big as Lord North that morning, but we showed 'em."

"Tootled a huntin' call at us, they did, they was that scornful," said another, "but pretty soon we was the hounds and *they* was the scared red foxes."

For Joel the test was still to come—any minute now. Since he had returned to the Army, there had been no fighting in which the Connecticut brigades took part. Washington had pulled out of the trap of Manhattan to Westchester. The group here on Chadderton's Hill was an outpost of the main Army camped in the valley below between rough wooded ridges and the narrow, meandering Bronx River.

A few yellow leaves drifted in idle grace from the trees; the wind smelled of apples and burning leaves. Starlings, camped overnight in the flaming maples, made a busy twittering; branches sprang upward as the whole flock took off at once. The birds knew the British were approaching many minutes before the men lying in wait behind the stone walls on the hilltop could see them.

"Here they come!" cried a soldier, as a long winding bright-colored snake began to creep through a gap in the tawny slopes. "Look at them horses prancing, will you?"

Joel, busy loading his musket, whispered to Denis, "I feel like I had the ague!"

"Don't we all of us?" Denis answered.

83

As from seats in an amphitheater, they saw the columns advance and a detachment of Colonials march out from the main camp to meet them. They could see the little puffs of smoke issuing from the gun barrels and hear the shots echoing through the valley. The Americans, outnumbered, soon fell back to the river, forded it, and began to climb the slopes of Chadderton's Hill. From the rear, an officer on horseback was urging them on. At the stream his horse reared and fell, floundering and splashing in the shallows, but the rider, still holding the bridle, scrambled to the bank.

"Lord save us," cried one of the officers on the hill, "the Hessians will take Ben Tallmadge unless we stop them. Give them everything you've got, boys!"

Joel jerked up his gun; the sound of it was lost in the blaze of musketry from all the others. The wall of Hessians crumbled and scattered. A cheer went up from the American lines as Tallmadge was seen to mount his horse and gallop off between the two armies to safety.

But the Hessian ranks came on like waves out of the sea; as soon as one crashed, another advanced from behind it. The Americans on the hill were outnumbered three to one. Joel went on loading and firing with no thought but to help wipe out a plague. Soon he had only a few of his fifteen balls left. But he felt cheated when the order was given to retire.

That night in camp at White Plains, he squatted on the ground, cleaning his musket and whistling like a veteran. Denis offered him a swig of rum. Joel refused; he felt drunk already.

"Feeling mighty pleased with yourself, ain't you, Red?"

84

Denis said. "I don't see anything so all-fired cheerful about the licking we took today."

"Denis, my friend, weren't you frightened when you were first fighting?" Joel asked.

"I was that scared I didn't know which way my hair stood," Denis said. "Still am, betimes, but it's a comfort to know that nobody is knowing it but me."

Joel nodded. "I was very afraid of being a coward again. But it doesn't matter, so long as you do what you should. That is why I am pleased—because I have learned this."

They rolled up in their blankets but Joel could not sleep. He looked at his hands, grimy with gunpowder, and thought that no one could call them the white useless hands of a scholar any longer. He was no longer one who talked and did nothing. Then suddenly his feeling of pleasure vanished and he seemed to see another sort of stain on his hands.

"What's up, Joe?" Denis asked sleepily. "What is it you're muttering away to yourself instead of sleeping?"

"I have read too much in the Scriptures," Joel said. "Sometimes passages come upon me at the wrong time."

"Recite what it is that's bothering you and I'll use it as a lullaby," Denis said. "There's been many a time in Church that the Holy Word has put me to sleep."

Joel moved restlessly, scuffling the dried leaves that were his bed, and spoke the verse that had been flaming before his eyes as vividly as if the page were lit up there in the darkness. " 'And the Lord said unto Cain, Where is Abel, thy brother? And he said, I know not; am I my brother's keeper?' "

"And are them paid murderers, the Hessians, your brothers?" Denis asked.

"I don't know. All men are, in the sight of God."

Denis, growing sleepier, grunted impatiently. "Say, Joe, it ain't against your religion to fight, is it?"

"Not any more than it's against yours. Did not your Jesus say that one should turn the other cheek?"

Denis rolled his blanket tighter against the autumn frost and murmured drowsily, "What you need, Joe me boy, is some callouses on your soul. Sure and you can't go through life always worrying about this and that. You'll worry your own self to death if you do, without any help from an English bullet."

9.

1777

"THIS be where I turn inland for Danbury," the teamster said. "Reckon you won't have no trouble though catching a ride to New Haven from here."

Joel thanked him and hobbled over to lean on the rail of the bridge that spanned a tidal river swirling out toward the Sound between wooded banks and brown marshes flecked with melting snow. He managed his crutch awkwardly; though his wound was healing, it was still painful.

For five months he had been a soldier, retreating with Washington's Army through Westchester and Jersey and into Pennsylvania, abandoning supplies and tents and guns. October, November, December. No winter uniforms or greatcoats, little food and most of it rotten. Officers told their men that citizens' hoarding and soaring prices were the reasons why Congress didn't take better care of their fighting men. You can't eat excuses, nor do they keep you warm, said Joel's comrades.

Men deserted right and left, but Joel was more convinced than ever of the need to fight. In all those months there had been only two victories: Trenton, where Washington had crossed the Delaware at Christmas time, and Princeton in January. At Princeton Joel had received a charge of grape in the leg, and now, after weeks of pain and fever, he had been invalided home.

He leaned on the bridge rail and watched a covey of chubby little black-and-white ducks dive and bob up again. As soon as his leg was better, he would re-enlist, he told himself. He did not see how he would have the patience to return to Jacob's store while the issue of the Revolution was in doubt. For all that he had no joy in soldiering, he had wanted to see this war through to its end.

The teamster had said the little cluster of houses around the bridge was a village on the outskirts of Fairfield. There was no cart or other conveyance to be seen on the road; Joel, shivering in the raw wind, decided to warm himself at the tavern and make inquiries there.

Fairfield was the town that had been young Abner's home, Joel remembered. "Do you know a family of the name of Bailie?" he asked the tavern keeper over a mug of hot flip.

"Squire Bailie of Compo? Sure do. Be he a friend of yours?"

"I was with the son Abner when he died."

"And you never met his folks? The Squire set a heap of store by the boy; he'd certainly appreciate it if you stopped in to see him."

"You don't think I would intrude?"

"You'd be doing the family a favor." The tavern keeper

88

glanced at Joel's crutch, leaning against the back of the oaken chair. "It ain't far from here, but futher than you'd find easy to walk. Let me send you down the river in the dory with my boy."

Joel hesitated, awkward and guilty that he had not made such a visit sooner, as he had promised.

"Do you know Abigail, the daughter?" the publican asked.

"I only saw her once."

The tavern keeper chuckled. "She's a whole petticoat army in herself, is Abby. A while back, she and some other young ladies threatened a Tory woman with a coat of molasses and feathers because she'd baptized her child Thomas Gage, after the Royal Governor of Boston town. The woman was so frighted, she changed the baby's name to George Washington right off. Abby's got a lot of spirit—but she's a modest, dutiful maid too."

Joel nodded thoughtfully over the rim of his mug. "If you can really spare your boy to take me, I think I will make that visit to Squire Bailie," he said.

At the mouth of the Saugatuck River, where it widened to a shallow estuary and a long peninsula pointed toward lonely reefs and the far blue shore of Long Island, the tavern keeper's boy pointed out a path leading up from the bank through the marsh grass. From the Bailie house, a few hundred yards back, you could no longer see the Sound, but you sensed that it was not far away. The clapboards were silvered with salt spray; gulls wheeled above the massive stone chimney; the apple trees in the orchard were twisted and windblown. There was a tang in the air of brine, salt hay, and mud flats. The plowed fields behind the barn made a neat brown

89

oasis in a wilderness of bayberry, tangled underbrush and cedar trees.

Abigail Bailie opened the door at Joel's knock. Two years had changed the moppet into a young maiden, but there was no mistaking the startling dark lashes and white-blond curls. She looked at him with puzzled eyes, taking in the soldier's hat with its feather, the crutch, and the bandaged leg. "I am Joel Davidov," he told her. "I was with your brother Abner in the Boston prison, and I promised there I would deliver for him a message to you."

"Of course," she said. "You are the one who wrote us of Abner, and we always hoped you would appear one day to tell us more. Come in, come in and sit down," she added hastily, putting out a small capable hand, sunburned even in winter, to ease him over the threshold. "Is it bad, the wound?"

"Not too bad any longer, but the surgeon said I could do no more soldiering for now."

Abigail led him to the settle by the hearth where a fire of applewood was smoldering, and went to call her parents from the adjoining chamber. Squire Bailie was a big, broad-shouldered man with a lined, balding forehead and humorous eyes. Abigail took after her mother, in whom, however, the slenderness was angular, the blond hair faded and pulled tight under her starched cap. As Joel told of Abner's long illness and his courage, Mistress Bailie sat erect at her spinning, a look of rigid composure on her finely carved face with its high-bridged nose, hollow cheeks, and thin firm lips. Abigail was perched on the arm of her father's chair, and in the chimney corner opposite, with one bony shank wrapped round the other, sat Gurdon, a gangling thirteen-year-old.

At the end of Joel's story, the father cleared his throat and blew his nose vigorously. "God be praised that we still have two children with us," he said. "Many families have lost more than one son already."

Gurdon unwound himself and began to prowl about the room. "It is time I volunteered in Abner's place," he said, in a voice which ran from squeak to croak and back again.

Mistress Bailie's spinning wheel jerked to a stop and her face was hidden over the broken thread.

But Abigail rushed to fling her arms around her brother. "No, Gurdy, no! You are too young. You shall not go!"

"Gurdon may be young but his sentiments do him proud, Abigail," said her father.

"I know—but Abner was too young, and now he is dead—and it was I who goaded him into it!" Abigail choked.

Squire Bailie patted her shoulder. "My son died for the things we all believe in—and if you had some part in hastening his departure, you should not chide yourself because of it."

"Abner was a good soldier and he was not afraid to die," Joel said softly. "That is what he wanted I should tell his family."

Gurdon was still brooding. "There are plenty as young as I in the war, aren't there?" he said to Joel.

"A few—they are brave but they don't have a man's strength. Drummer boys, they are mostly."

"Gurdy—you who wish to be a minister of the gospel!" Abigail said. "Would you throw away your studies, to be a drummer boy?"

"I am sick of studying when others are fighting." Gurdon kicked rebelliously at the stones of the chimney corner.

Joel regarded him with sympathy. "I, too, had this to decide. But I am older. Believe me, it will be better to wait."

"Do you intend to be a minister also, young man?" Bailie asked.

"I am a Jew, Squire Bailie," Joel answered. "I had thought to be a rabbi, yes. With our people, the rabbi is not a priest, not a parson, but only a teacher."

He felt that the Bailies were staring; the silence after his remark seemed overly long. This little family was so secure, so snug and comfortable in a house their forebears had inhabited for over a hundred years. The hand-hewn beams and plastered walls, the mellow pine chests and tables, the braided mats on the wide, scrubbed floorboards, all spoke of a home loved and well-cared for, one that did not have to be abandoned each few generations to seek a new home in a distant land. The long-barreled musket over the fireplace was the only reminder of a less settled day.

He felt the red rising unbidden to his cheeks. Sometimes he thought it would be easier to look the way most people here seemed to think a Jew should, with black hair, a hooked nose, and a beard. In Poland you did not have to make such an announcement; there were plenty of red-haired, blue-eyed Jews, and besides, you lived in a ghetto.

Mistress Bailie's foot resumed its steady beat on the treadle of the spinning wheel; logs crackled on the hearth, and the February wind moaned in the chimney breast. "New Haven is where your family lives, young man?" said Squire Bailie. "That is a good ways from here and it is nigh on sunset. Will you not honor us by spending the night? Then when we have supped, we can speak more of Abner, and of the things you have seen in the Army. I should like to hear of them."

He was obviously sincere, and Joel was very tired. He accepted gratefully. After a supper of cold meat and Indian pudding, washed down with mugs of cool cider, they talked for a little while. Then Squire Bailie picked up the big family Bible which lay handy on the table. "You know the Hebrew tongue, I presume?"

"Why shouldn't I?" Joel answered.

"Each morning and each evening before we retire I read aloud a chapter from the Scriptures," Squire Bailie said. "This night you shall do it, if you will—translating the passages into the Hebrew as you read."

Joel turned to the opening of Genesis, holding the book close to the light of the fire. "In the beginning God created the heaven and the earth," he began in English and then, substituting the Hebrew words, read the chapter through.

" 'And God saw everything that He had made, and behold it was very good,' " Squire Bailie intoned, when Joel had ended. "I do not know if your scholarship is correct, but you seem quick and fluent." He walked over to warm his back by the fire. "All parsons should learn Hebrew; it is the key to the Scriptures. It is taught at Harvard for that purpose, but how can we afford to send Gurdon there in times like these?" He turned to his son. "Let us ask this young man to remain with us a while, so that he may instruct you in the language."

Gurdon stammered that he would be pleased with the arrangement—if Joel would tutor him in the manual of arms as well.

"Perhaps you have other plans?" Bailie said to Joel.

"I had thought to return to my brother-in-law's shop in New Haven, but I can't say the prospect interests me."

"Then stay with us," Bailie said. "I am not a rich man; I can pay you only a pittance, but in addition you would have free lodging and my good wife's victuals to put some meat on those bones."

The mistress of the house said, "It would give me great pleasure to have Abner's friend in our household."

Joel was touched by her words. To live with a Gentile family would be a new experience for him. He might learn much of the ways of this country. "I only hope you will be pleased with my teaching," he said.

"Well, then, it is settled." Bailie stretched and yawned. "It is time for all God-fearing folk to seek their repose. Come with me, young man, and I will show you where you are to lodge. It is an attic room, but clean and comfortable."

As winter drew to an end, Poland seemed very far away in time and space to Joel, and the war almost as distant. After the victories at Trenton and Princeton, the British had retired to New York, leaving almost all of Jersey in Washington's hands. The Army went into winter quarters on Morristown Heights, and the fighting was over for the season; people, both at home and abroad, began to say that Washington was a pretty good general.

Western Connecticut was rich farm country; the mills along the Saugatuck and Mill River and Ash Creek ground wheat flour, cornmeal and buckwheat for the Army; pork butts and sausages were smoked in the barnyards; saltpeter was collected for gunpowder. Connecticut Yankees worked hard for the war and had sent many of their sons to the Army. But there had been no actual fighting on Connecticut soil, and they felt the pinch of war little as yet. The Bailie family ate from wooden trenchers, having given their pewter for bullets, but the trenchers were piled high with nourishing food; meat pies, baked beans, fish from the Sound, puddings sweetened with maple sugar and honey.

The food, the rest and comforts did wonders for Joel; his leg mended fast. The work with Gurdon went well; Joel enjoyed teaching and he was pleasantly surprised to discover how well-grounded in the Scriptures the boy already was. He had not realized that the Bible was the only book in many New England homes, and served as history, literature, and a guide to behavior. And since the New Testament had been distorted by the Stuart kings to gain the unlimited submission of their subjects, the Puritans had turned to the Old Testament for their laws and political ideas.

"I think very fitting the seal proposed for our new government by Mr. Adams, Mr. Jefferson and Dr. Franklin," Squire Bailie said. "It represents the Exodus of the Israelites, with Moses causing the Red Sea to overwhelm Pharaoh's army, and it bears the legend, 'Rebellion to tyrants is Obedience to God.' The English speak of the Divine Right of kings; they have forgotten that God Alone is King."

"And where His Spirit is, there is liberty," Abigail put in. For all her harum-scarum ways, Abigail was intensely serious about two things: her religion and the patriot cause. Joel loved to hear her hold forth; her cheeks would get so red and her voice would rise far above the gentle tones be-fitting a maiden.

"Liberty is not license," her mother would remind her. "Abigail, have you done your chores today?"

Abigail would nod her head so vigorously that her dimity cap bobbed up and down. "I have pickled and preserved; I have swept and scrubbed and ironed." Or she would say that she had spun linen and spooled and carded wool for soldiers' coats—"I have been Liberty daughter enough for today! Come, Joel, let us go out on the river."

"Very well," Joel would answer, "but I am going to do the rowing. A girl shouldn't work so heavily when a man is here—even though you are wonderfully strong. And I don't need two whole legs for pulling at oars."

She would walk beside him to the shore, slowing her light impatient steps to his halting gait, chattering of how good it was to be out in the spring wind, not cramped within walls. Sometimes light hearted, sometimes (when she spoke of God or country) ardently serious—was there ever so variable a maiden? But she was a good comrade, almost like a younger sister to him.

10.

NOW IT was April; the willow boughs wore a lime-colored fuzz; green shoots were pushing up between the sere stalks of the rushes; peepers sang in the ponds at twilight. Winter was over; animals and soldiers were coming out of their winter quarters, and soon the summer campaigns would be under way. Connecticut folk were busy adding to the stockpile of army supplies in the magazine at Danbury.

One day toward the end of the month, Squire Bailie went to New Haven on legal business, taking Gurdon with him. So Joel was free of his tutorial duties; it was a mild sunny afternoon, and Abigail asked him to go with her to make salt, of which there was a great scarcity. He had long ago discarded his crutch for a cane, and by now was agile enough to help carry the big kettle to the beach. They waded barefooted into the water to fill it, Abigail holding up her skirts and squealing at the cold. The kettle was hung over a fire of driftwood which smelled sweet and pungent as incense. While they waited for the sea water to boil away, they sat idly watching the brisk little sandpipers that skittered along the wet sand, bobbing and pecking at tidbits.

Joel stretched out his feet to warm them at the fire, while Abby dried hers with her petticoat and modestly tucked them beneath her skirts. She reached over and gently traced the angry purple scar than ran along his shin. When she looked up, her hazel eyes were pained and guilty. "I am ashamed of the names I called you that day in New London—before I knew you. I was a dreadful creature, wasn't I?"

"Tory-lover, you called me—and even now I do not think one must be wicked to be a Loyalist. But you, Abby, never doubted from the first, did you?"

"Never!" said Abigail. Her eyes sparkled and the words tumbled out. "I do not see how anyone could fail to believe in the words of our great Declaration: that all men, even the poorest and meanest, are born with equal rights!"

"Even a Jew?"

"Of course!" Abigail cried. "You carry a chip on your shoulder, Joel—always daring someone to knock it off. We know many Jews in Norwalk, most respected merchants. You are as good as anyone in this Commonwealth."

"Not quite," Joel said. "Not yet." The Connecticut charter declared the Christian faith to be, "the only and principal end of the plantation"; this made a nonchurch member, to some degree, an outlaw. "Perhaps, Abby, when the war is over, and there is a new country, religions and politics will not be mixed up together. That is what should be and it's

98

one reason why I fight." He corrected himself. "Why I did fight."

"Do you want to fight again some day, when your leg mends?" Abigail asked.

"Of course. You would approve, Abby—yes?"

She looked away. "I—I no longer advise what anyone should do. Each must decide for himself. But I think you have done enough. . . . The water must be boiled away by now; it is growing late." She jumped up and offered her hand to help Joel rise.

He did not like always to be helped. With the aid of his stick, he got to his feet by his own efforts, and before picking up the kettle, turned for a last look at the sunset-colored water and the Norwalk Islands bleak and dark against it. Long Island, this afternoon, was blue and unnaturally close; natives called this a sign of rain. He stared, and stared again. "Look, Abby, far out in the Sound—those ships—"

It was a fleet of sail, more than a score of them.

"Our ships, Joel?"

"They are too far away to tell—but we haven't such a big squadron near here. British, I think, bound for their base at Newport probably. But look—they are altering their course. Almost one might think they were coming here!"

Abigail's hand went to her throat and her breath fluttered as they watched the ships come about, trim sails, and appear to be standing in for the very spot on which they stood. Nearer and nearer they came, rounding the reefs off Cockenoe Island, furling topsails and slacking sheets so that there could be no doubt that they were heading for the mouth of the Saugatuck.

99

"British ships of war, there's no longer any question. It is an invasion," Joel said, in a tumult of mixed feelings: fear for Abigail's safety and his own, regret that the peace of the winter, however false, was over, and a rising, renewed hatred of those who came from the Old World with their hired soldiers to stamp out the brave spirit of his American neighbors.

"What shall we do, Joel?" Abigail cried. "What can they possibly want in our little village?"

"Nothing good, that's sure. We must warn the people, tell the Coast Guard in case they haven't seen these ships yet. You can run, Abby, so go—go quickly and tell them."

"And you?"

"I will stay a little while to watch what happens."

Abigail picked up her skirts to run, but still she did not move. "Joel—don't let them take you!"

"Don't fear. I have had enough of British prisons. If the Lobsters come near, I fly home like a bird."

Even as Abby's feet scattered the sand of the beach path, the alarm bells began to ring. The enemy fleet was rounding up in the lee of Cockenoe and coming to anchor; close enough for Joel to count the number of vessels. There were twenty-six of them, big ships of war and bulky transports, enough to carry an army of several thousand men. Across the water the sounds carried startlingly clear: rattle of anchor chains paying out, slap of canvas as sails were furled. The bosun's pipe shrilled orders, and men began to swarm over the sides like a string of moving beads. Horses too were being whipped into the landing barges; there would be cavalry to reckon with. Joel hobbled away in a hurry.

He found Abigail and her mother standing close together at the window. The sudden night of early spring had fallen; the glare of soldiers' campfires was already reflecting up from the beach. "You are not going to stay here, surely?" he asked.

"I do not believe they have come to conquer petticoats," Abigail's mother said, and went, erect and unhurried as ever, to answer a rap at the door. "Come in, come in, Neighbor Disbrow—it is good to have you back from the wars, even on a short furlough. No, my good man is not at home. Is there anything you wished of him?"

"We need every man who can carry a gun, young or old. You are aware of the British landing?"

"How could I help it? They have landed almost in my front yard."

"You had best pack up your valuables and fly, Mistress Bailie," the neighbor said.

"I will not desert my home," she answered sharply. "Why has the enemy come here to Compo? We are not rich gentry worth plundering."

"This squadron is commanded by Major General Tryon— an English gentleman so noted for his barbarism that when he governed North Carolina, even the Indians called him 'Great Wolf.' The British have a way of thinking that the more helpless folk they frighten, the fewer patriots there will be. They don't understand that here in America, such tactics have the opposite effect."

Indeed they had, Joel thought. If it had not been for Major General Tryon perhaps he would not have awakened yet from his pleasant little dream—the dream that he could relax for a while, till his leg was mended—but once the dogs of war were roused, sooner or later they came for you. He went to the chimney breast to take down the flintlock that hung there, the powder horn and bullet pouch.

Abigail tried to wrest them from him, crying, "No, Joel; you must not go with Captain Disbrow. Your leg is scarcely healed; you will do fresh damage to it!"

"Isn't a musket as good to lean on as an oaken stick?" he asked, laughing at how she tried to boss him.

"Our young tutor is right," said her mother, "a little limp is no cause for pampering." Abigail shot her an angry look.

Captain Disbrow and Joel were the only ones among the Minute Men gathered at the tavern who had seen service with the real army. "Boys," Disbrow said, "there are mighty few of us to stop two thousand British. All we can do is delay them till the militia comes from other towns. I figure the best place to wait in ambush is Compo Road, which they're bound to pass coming from Cedar Point. Anyone got a better suggestion?"

They were all agreed, so they shouldered their guns and went stealthily to hide behind a stone wall on the road leading to the beach. In the moonlight it lay white as if winter snow still covered it, and the black shadows of the trees, wavering in the spring wind, danced on it like witches. The moon had a great hazy ring around it and sometimes blurred quite away; the shadows came and went. Joel crouched against the cold damp stones, straining his ears for sound, hearing nothing but the young frogs singing, and a night heron's distant "quawk, quawk!"

"Quawk, quawk!" Disbrow answered unexpectedly, and a

moment later a scout slipped through the shrubs and dropped down by his side. "They're a-coming," he said.

Disbrow stood up. "At night, like this, it's got to be mighty close before you can see enough to shoot good. Hold your fire and make every bullet count."

Now they could hear the jingle of harness, the rhythmic tramp of feet on ground still hard with the winter's frost. The British marched with flying banners and no attempt to hide, for they knew themselves to be King George's crack soldiers, the flower of his army. First in line was the Yorkshire Regiment which had beaten the Americans at Brooklyn; then the Royal Welsh Fusiliers, veterans of Bunker Hill. The brass fieldpieces of the artillery and the bright trappings of the horsemen glittered. Yellow buckskin breeches and polished black knee boots, spotless white facings on coats dark as dried blood; and under the glistening helmets decorated with death's heads and nodding plumes, the faces, white and hollow-eyed in the moonlight, looked like death's heads too.

The Minute Men lay behind the stone wall and watched the procession come on. They knew their first volley would draw an answer, and there wasn't much chance that they'd survive it.

"As soon as you've fired, get back from the wall and scatter," Disbrow whispered; "that way maybe we'll live to hit 'em by surprise again some other place. Ready, boys?"

The flintlocks cocked in chorus.

"Who goes there?" shouted the British major.

"You will know soon!" Disbrow answered. And the muskets spoke.

103

The major's horse, snorting with fear, reared and fell over backward. Behind him, men toppled like tenpins; those still standing let go a volley and an American boy, running for the shelter of the woods, spun about and fell. But the whole British line was thrown into confusion; horses plunging and trying to bolt, men screaming, officers yelling orders to bring up carts from the rear for the wounded. By the time discipline was restored, the Minute Men had lost themselves in the brush.

When the enemy column had resumed its march, Captain Disbrow counted noses. One of his brave friends was dead and another wounded. There seemed little use in trying a second attack on a whole army. The Minute Men voted to go home to guard their women.

A fine Friday evening this had been, Joel thought; Sabbath peace had been the furthest thing from his mind. He slept that night across the doorsill for fear of stragglers. Next day he learned that Tryon's troops had camped overnight to the north of Fairfield and seemed to be on their way to Danbury.

Stiff and lame he hobbled restlessly from house to river's edge and back, and back and forth again, eyeing the squadron at anchor. Sunlight winked on brass deck cannon as the ships of war swung with the tide, looking like little models of ships, newly carved and neatly painted. As long as they waited here in the mouth of the Saugatuck, Tryon was bound to come this way again.

Joel rowed to the tavern by the bridge to learn the latest news. All day fugitives came panting in to tell their tales over bumpers of ale. Tryon had breakfasted with a Tory in

Redding; he was approaching Danbury; the little garrison there had been forced to retreat. The invaders had broken open the magazine and destroyed everything: tents, uniforms, ammunition, food. The streets of Danbury were said to be ankle deep in spilled liquor and melted fat from burned pork and beef. And the Hessians were running riot through the town.

"But Gold Silliman's comin' with the milishy," said the men at the tavern, banging their mugs on the tables. "By Glory, we'll make the Wolf run with his tail between his legs!"

Squire Bailie and Gurdon returned that evening with the news that General Silliman and General Arnold were on the march toward Danbury with large forces of men. But next morning it was raining so hard that any battle action must be bogged down.

"And we can't do anything but wait?" Joel said. "It seems to me that is all we do."

"True enough. God send us patience to bear it."

Early the next day the summons came to the men of the West Parish. A smoke signal had been seen to the north, near Ridgefield. Tryon was on his way back, burning houses as he came.

Squire Bailie took the musket and Joel a fowling piece that stood in a corner. Gurdon scowled. "What weapon is left for me?"

"You must stay here, my son," said his father.

"With the *women*?"

"You will have to guard the women, Gurdon," Joel said. "This is most important."

"Abigail is quite able to take care of herself," Gurdon said sulkily. "If I were a Redcoat, I wouldn't want to stand up to her." He pointed to Joel, "Why shouldn't *he* stay behind? Look at him. He can hardly walk."

"But I can shoot, Gurdon," Joel said gently. "In this I have experience that helps—and you have not. A brave man—Nathan Hale—you know him—said to me once, 'You will have time to fight later. The war is not over.'"

They left Gurdon, unconsoled, and rowed the boat to the bridge which was the mustering place, where were gathered, not just a few Minute Men but over five hundred militia, some regulars and part of an artillery company. Enough anyway to give Tryon a good fight. And he was not far away; already one could hear the crackle of musketry: Colonial troops posted on a hill were greeting the enemy column as it came down the road from Danbury.

Joel sprinkled powder in the flashpan of his gun, dropped powder and a leaden ball into the barrel and rammed them home. The British would have to pass over this bridge in order to reach the side of the river which led to the beach and their landing craft. The bridge made a fine Lobster trap, said one of the militia men.

Then a shout of angry disappointment went up. The Redcoats had forded the stream well above the bridge and were trotting along the far bank out of range of American fire.

The militia men poured over the bridge and pelted after them with wild yells. The British, well in the lead, made for the high hill of Compo, dragged up their field cannon and trained them at the oncoming Americans. It was a strong

106

position, and behind it the far slope lay open to the landing place.

General Arnold led the assault on the hill. Joel toiled up the slope. Behind him a cracked voice said with embarrassment, "Do you know how one goes about loading a blunderbuss?"

"Good heavens, Gurdon!" Joel cried. "How did you come here—and where did you get that thing?" For Gurdon was staggering under a huge rusty gun which had not seen service since the French Wars.

"In the attic," Gurdon said, and added with dignity. "Why should I not be here? The women are safe enough behind barred doors. Am I not even allowed to come to the defense of my own home?"

This Joel felt he could not deny, knowing how he himself felt. "The gun will explode if you try to fire it," he explained to Gurdon, hurrying on. But Gurdon dogged his footsteps.

A blast of cannonball and grapeshot came from the hilltop, and the militia men wavered as many fell wounded. Then a young lieutenant, climbing on a wall, shouted, "For God's sake, men, don't retreat. Don't run. Let's march up the hill and drive them off!" For a moment he stood there, a rash and gallant figure, but even as the men pressed forward, he staggered and fell. A Hessian leaped over the fence with a bayonet poised to make a finish of him. Gurdon flung the heavy blunderbuss. The German went down with guttural cries. Joel glanced around and saw Gurdon, leaning against a tree, being sick. He took a moment to go to him.

Gurdon looked up at him with guilty eyes. "Was it wrong, what I did?"

"No, Gurdon. War is war. Logically one cannot be fussy about the method of it. While you are fighting, you must try to drive the things you see out of your mind."

"I can't," Gurdon gasped. "I don't think I ever will."

"Later one ought to remember how horrified one felt, but very few people do," Joel said bitterly.

Boatloads of fresh marines were coming in from the ships to hold the position on the hill. The battle-weary Redcoats and Hessians straggled down the far slope to embark, a very different group from the smart soldiers who had landed at this same spot three nights before. They stumbled and weaved as they ran, many of them still foggy on the rum they had swilled. They were red-eyed and filthy. They had destroyed the stores laid up for Washington's hungry army, but they had also overstuffed their own bellies in Danbury. And many had been wounded, in today's fighting and at Ridgefield the day before, where the Americans had caught up with them. Even the officers seemed bewildered and uncertain. Joel knew that they did not understand how hundreds of fighting men could be raised from these peaceful farms and villages overnight. No one born in Europe could at first understand these Yankees who didn't fight for the love of fighting, or for pay, or even because they were pressed into service like the British soldiers. Men who whooped like savage Indians, battled like demons, and quoted the Bible as they fought.

But even these men were tired now, and still outnumbered. By sunset the British had managed to evacuate the hill and ferry out to the transports all their men but the dead and wounded left on the ground. Just as it was growing dark, the ships up-anchored and glided away, bound across the Sound for the British stronghold at Huntington.

The Minute Men dispersed, some to their anxious wives and some to the taverns to celebrate with a bumper or two. Joel wearily limped toward the Bailies', grimacing because now that the excitement was over, he knew how his leg pained him. More painful than this was the memory of the sights he'd seen; like Gurdon he did not think he would ever be able to put out of his mind the mangled bodies, the lives thrown away, the men, lusty and young and whole, who would be half-men and cripples from this time on. Always, at the end of a day of killing, he felt guilty for his share in it. And then he would remind himself, as he did now, of a passage from one of Tom Paine's pamphlets: "Not all the treasures of the world, so far as I believe, could have induced me to support an offensive war, for I think it murder; but if a thief breaks into my house, burns and destroys my property, and threatens to kill me, or those that are in it, and to bind me in all cases whatsoever to his absolute will, am I to suffer it?"

It was dark and quiet now on the hill that had seen bloody confusion so short a time before. Suddenly a fiery signal leaped into the darkness from a high rock—tar barrels set ablaze as a send-off to the enemy. The forked crimson tongue danced and the turgid black smoke billowed above it; the smell of burning tar mingled with the fading odors of battle: gunpowder and blood—and the clean fresh smell of the marshes. This was the Yankee answer to Tryon: "You may burn our homes and destroy the arms with which we fight," the leaping flames proclaimed, "but when you run away, we'll still be here—free men!" And a ship of the British squadron, confused by the new beacon, went aground on the reefs of Cockenoe.

Abigail burst out of the house at the sound of Joel's lame step. "Here, lean on me!" she cried. "Gurdon is already here, and I am *so* vexed with him! He might have been killed if you had not stopped him from trying to use that dreadful old gun."

"You should not blame your brother for showing spirit," he smiled. "After all, you so admire this!"

She sighed. "I am so confused. I think men should fight for the cause, and then, when those I love are in danger, I cannot bear it!"

Yes, Abigail was very attached to Gurdon, Joel thought.

"Oh, I am so glad you are home!" she went on. "Come quickly into the house. Whether you like it or not, I am going to put a poultice on your leg."

"If you would like to do it, I would like this very much," Joel said. And thought, as he entered the door with her, how good it was to hear Abby speak as if the Bailie house were his home too.

11.

THE Bailies had first welcomed Joel as their dead son Abner's friend; now, having helped to defend the home, he was accepted wholeheartedly as a member of it. His leg was healing, and he began to do chores which had been neglected since the worthless Alf Hodges had been dismissed. Squire Bailie was only part a farmer; most of his time was spent in the practice of law in Fairfield, the shire town of the county. So he was glad to have Joel care for the barnyard animals, the pigs and hens and the riding horse. The Warsaw years had left Joel starved for the green fields of his childhood; in him there was a large strain of the Biblical Jews who rejoiced in Canaan, the land of milk and honey. Under his care the sandy West Parish soil produced more maize and squash and beans than ever before.

Outwardly, though he was not aware of it, he began more
and more to resemble his neighbors, as his skin took on a
ruddy tan well-dusted with freckles. The accent faded from
his speech, though he still sometimes gave words a different
twist. Like many of the younger American Jews, he had
abandoned some of the traditional orthodox observances.
He did not ask for specially prepared dishes while in a Gentile house, though he still would not eat flesh of the pig. It
was a difficult temptation to avoid when succulent smoked
hams and sausages appeared on the table. He acknowledged
God with the same faith as ever, but ritual, he thought, was
the least important part of religion. There was so much in
the New England way of life: the reading of the Old Testament, the grace before meals, the very laws of the Commonwealth, similar to the doctrines of his own people, that it was
easy to fit in.

The people of the parish too accepted him now as a neighbor, slightly different from themselves, but no longer a queer
stranger of doubtful virtue. When Abigail went to a spinning-
wheel party, where the Daughters of Liberty competed over
who could spin the most wool for the Army, she insisted that
Joel come at the close of it with the other young men to drink
a berry-brew called Labrador tea and to serenade the girls
with Liberty songs.

"Don't pretend you cannot sing," she said, "for I have
heard you when you were weeding the garden patch. Of
course I could not understand the words, but you have a fine
hearty voice, Joel."

So, stammering a little at first, he sang along with the
others:

"Come join hand in hand, brave Americans all,
And rouse your bold hearts at fair Liberty's call,
No tyrannous act shall suppress your just claim
Nor stain with dishonor America's name."

Afterward he would carry home for Abby the small spinning wheel she used for such occasions. No other young man was sparking her, she declared; she kept them all at arm's length.

It was a busy pleasant life, but Joel was restless. While he was comfortably housed and well fed, Fort Ticonderoga, the main defense against invasion from Canada, had fallen, and General Burgoyne was marching down through New England with Indian allies who burned homes, scalped and killed old people, women and children. Joel had had a pleasant holiday from the grim business of war but he could no longer enjoy it, hearing these tales. Everywhere the militia was being aroused.

When he volunteered, however, the recruiting officer turned him down. "You couldn't make long marches, much less run for it, with that leg of yours. Stick to the home guard, young feller."

Joel turned away bitterly and went to neighboring Black Rock, for he had heard that Matt Barry was there captaining one of the whaleboats which made frequent raids on the Tories of Long Island.

"Glad to see you, lad; I sure wondered what the Boston Provost done to you, all on account o' me." He told Joel that he had been kept on a prison hulk in Boston Harbor until the siege was lifted; then, like Joel, he had been released.

"They didn't give us much to eat, did they? But you look hearty enough."

"I am strong like an ox and sick of being treated as a cripple because I limp a little," Joel said. "I want you to take me on for that seagoing militia of yours. I can pull an oar, lame or not."

"I reckon you can shoot too, since you was in the Army long enough to get wounded," Matt Barry said. "How far can you walk on your game leg? Five miles?"

"Far enough," Joel said.

So he went with Captain Matt on his raids, crossing the Sound at night, pouncing on a supply depot, burning some shipping, or fodder intended for the British Army, capturing a few horses, kidnaping a Tory or two in reprisal for similar raids made by the other side. Gurdon had joined the Coast Guard that nightly patrolled the beaches, and he slept half the days after he had been on duty. So Joel, when he was not off with Captain Matt, had spare time which Abigail came often to spend with him. Whenever her indoor chores would permit it, she would help him with the farm duties, picking sweet corn and late summer squash, gathering the salt hay he had scythed for mulching the garden, turning over the soil for next spring's planting. He would sift the sandy loam through his fingers sometimes and wonder, was this at last the soil of his home, his native land? Surely his mother had been wrong in saying that Jews would never be able to claim any soil of their own till they came home from their wanderings to *Eretz Israel*, the land of Israel. That was too long to wait. And the longer he lived in America, the more he felt that the ideals of its people were similar to his own.

As they worked, Joel told Abigail stories of the ghetto in Poland, of the poverty and hardship, the festivals that were solemn, and those that were happy. He told her of student days in Warsaw, and of that other rebellion in his boyhood. Pulaski, his old hero, was now an officer with General Washington, carrying on the same fight for freedom. "While I enjoy myself in the lovely sunshine," Joel said. "This petty banditry of Captain Matt's is not enough to do. My leg is healed; it has been weeks at least since I have felt even a twinge."

"Are you *sure?*" she asked. One might almost think she did not wish him to join up again. But that was impossible; Abigail was so ardent a patriot.

He found as the days went by that he wished more and more to be with her; when she was absent on nationly duties, a sewing bee or a society where the maidens made paper cartridges of powder and ball, he missed her tomboy ways, her attempts to boss him, her bright hair and the odd, dark-fringed hazel eyes. She meant to him the very spirit of the country he was coming to love so dearly, a younger spirit than his own because it was product of a younger civilization; a little unthinking at times, but refreshingly sure of itself.

He was no longer a child, not to know where his sentiments were leading him. And he thought that to love a Gentile maid—who could not possibly love him except in an offhand sisterly fashion—was a bitter thing. Yet still he lingered, hating to say good-by, reluctant to leave the Bailies who had made him so much a member of the family, reluctant also to leave his pupil Gurdon. Teaching, he found, was the thing that he most liked to do. It pleased him to point out to Gurdon that the principles of freedom and justice for which America was fighting were the same which the Jew had always held dear—and stemmed from the same source, the Old Testament. He was pleased—and somewhat astonished —to hear comment from the Bailies on the sermons of many a New England parson tracing the Western world's idea of democracy back to the principles set down by Moses.

"How much the ways of God toward us, His people of New England, are like His dealing with the ancient Israelites!" Gurdon would say, for instance. "They too lived under the rule of their gospel, defended by leaders chosen by themselves."

And yet Joel felt that he must no longer remain in Fairfield. The work on the garden was done. The scarlet and gold October leaves had drifted away; only the sere and yellow were left, and the carpet of brown beneath the trees. The snake-necked herons had left their fishing in the Saugatuck to fly South, and in their place, fleets of black ducks and mallards sailed among the eel grass. The Fall Pippins had been taken to the mill to be crushed into cider; the bayberries had been gathered and melted down for winter candles. It was November. And lately Abigail had taken to avoiding him. Perhaps, in spite of his effort to hide it, she suspected his love for her and was repulsed.

Joel went to Captain Matt. "I have had enough of this playing at war. You shall go to the recruiting officer with me to vouch that I am fit to be a soldier."

"I suppose you know what you're in for?" Matt Barry asked.

"I do not expect it will be an easy life," Joel said.

"Easy life is one thing. Marching without shoes on an empty belly—that's a far cry from it."

"I am tired of being companion to women and little boys," Joel said violently.

"Very well, lad, if that's what you want."

Willing soldiers were hard to come by that autumn. New England, after the surrender of General Burgoyne at Saratoga, seemed safe; Pennsylvania and the South were too distant for the Yankees to worry about. Thousands of enlistments were to expire with the New Year, and the recruiting officer knew very well that they would not be renewed. He hardly needed to be persuaded that Joel was able-bodied.

At supper that night, Joel told Squire Bailie that he was due to join the army at Peekskill in a week; meanwhile, on the morrow, he would return to his own family at New Haven. When he retired to his attic room, he could not sleep. After tomorrow he might never see Abigail again, or, when he did, she would be married to another. Abigail was no longer a moppet; she was almost seventeen and growing prettier each day. She had given a start and turned pale at his news; no doubt she was fond of him in a sisterly way, but that was no longer enough. He no longer wished to be tolerated as Abner's friend.

In his slant-ceilinged room, he was caged like a beast. He prowled the floor like a beast, longing to speak to Abigail, just once before he left, of his love for her. But no, the Puritan maid would not likely marry a Jew. And he refused to beg humbly for favors.

The room's one small window was nailed tight to keep out the winter. Joel felt cramped, imprisoned, surrounded by

117

strangers; he should have left this alien house long ago. Well, he would be going in the morning. Meanwhile, a breath of the open air might make sleep come easier.

A light snow had fallen earlier but the sky was now clear. Starlight glittered on the tall frosted tassels of the marsh grass. The drooping willows, each twig outlined in white, were a cascade of lacework. Unseen beyond the snow-powdered hummocks, the river sighed against the shore. A branch rustled, though there was no wind. A breath of vapor showed, though there was no mist. Shrinking behind the bare lilac bush by the doorstep was a small figure wrapped in a cloak red as sumac berries.

"Oh Joel—" Abigail's voice was choked.

"Abby! Why are you crying?"

She ran to him like a child seeking help; flung her arms around his neck, buried her head against his jacket. Joel stood rigid, telling himself, above the rush of feeling that overwhelmed him at her touch, that he must act the big brother and comfort whatever it was that ailed her. He lifted her face, trying to see in the starlight, what expression lurked there. Her hood fell back, and instead of searching her face, he covered it with kisses, on the wet cheeks, the troubled forehead, the flaxen hair that was downy like a baby's.

"I can't bear to have you go off to war again!" she sobbed.

"Abby, Abby," he chided, wondering that she did not hear his heart thumping, "and you such a patriot! You, out of all people to say this!"

"But I love you!" she answered indignantly.

For a moment he could not believe the words; it was as if the sun had suddenly risen, first blinding him and then making the whole cold world and the uncertain future warm with hope. In the wonder of it he clasped her so fiercely that she cried out. She was shivering; sobs still shook her as if to shake her apart. He moved away a step; when he could control himself, he drew her inside the house to the settle by the fire where the embers still glowed, sat down beside her and took her icy hands in his. She leaned back with closed eyes, the color coming and going in her cheeks. The thick lashes lifted and she smiled.

"That is better—it's not a catastrophe to love one another," he said, and added, his own doubts returning, "though things may be difficult for us two. Do you *know* what you said, Abigail? Are you sure it's not just that you are swept away because I'm going off again to be a soldier? That doesn't mean I'm a hero, you know."

"You *are* a hero to join up again," she said stubbornly. "You were wounded once; that's enough for anyone to do!"

He laughed. "Oh Abby, you're a baby sometimes. There are thousands like me, some that were much worse hurt and still they go on fighting. And if you think so highly of me, why did you avoid me lately?"

She hung her head. "I thought you didn't love me. You acted so—so brotherly. I thought you could love only a Jewess."

Joel shook his head. "We are a man and a woman; love pulls us together—shall we say no to our hearts? But your father," he said soberly, "maybe won't like to have a son-in-law that is a Jew?"

"What nonsense! He's said over and over again that men are born free and equal and that all men are brothers. And he likes you very much; he knows as well as I do how good and brave you are!"

"I'm not particularly either of those things. Anyhow liking me is different from having me as husband to his daughter. But I hope you're right—I will speak to him in the morning."

Squire Bailie strode up and down the room while Joel watched him with anxious eyes, waiting for his answer.

The older man paused and put his hand on Joel's shoulder. He cleared his throat. "You know that I respect you, Joel. Have I not treated you, these last months, almost as a son?"

"Indeed you have, sir, and I'm very grateful for your kindness."

"Well then, you must know that there is nothing personal in my hesitation. Of course, you should have asked my permission before courting Abigail—"

"The love came upon us before we knew," Joel apologized.

"Yes, yes—I should have realized that two young people, thrown together as you were, would be bound to fancy themselves in love. But a betrothal is not to be entered into lightly."

"What are your objections, sir? Is it that I am a Jew?"

Squire Bailie again cleared his throat uncomfortably. "It is not the religious difference that worries me—although you may find more conflicts with Abby over this than you expect. There are many problems when those who marry come from different backgrounds, with different ideas of conduct and customs. I am very fond of my daughter; I would not wish to see her made unhappy."

120

Joel, with his oversensitive reaction to any possible insult, stiffened. "What is there about my conduct which could make Abigail unhappy? I love her; naturally I would be kind to her always."

"I did not mean that," Squire Bailie said impatiently. "In this household we all know you to be a fine young fellow. But others—in the years to come—who knows what Abigail might have to face as the wife of a Jew? It may not be easy. Even in this country for which we have such high hopes of freedom and tolerance."

"It has never been easy to be a Jew," Joel said proudly. "Nevertheless I would not be anything else. Surely Abby knows this."

"She may know it and still not realize what it means," Squire Bailie said kindly. "At any rate, we must do nothing hasty. You are going off to the wars, my boy; who knows how long it may be before you return?"

"Or if I return at all," Joel said. "You are right, sir; I cannot ask a promise from Abby with such an uncertain future."

He went to fetch his portmanteau and make his good-byes to the rest of the family. "I will walk down the road with you a piece," Abby said.

Her mother, she told him stormily, had put even more difficulties in their way. "She says it is not only my happiness she is considering; that she is fond of you, and doesn't want to see either of us hurt. She asked, for instance," Abigail blushed scarlet, "how we would bring up our children—in your faith or mine?"

Children naturally took the religion of the father, Joel

thought, but there was no time to discuss this now. "For people like us there are many things to decide," he said. "You must think hard on them, dearest, as I do."

"You have doubts too?"

"Of course I have doubts. Not about loving you, or your loving me, but whether my way of life can make you happy."

"Haven't I always been happy with you—in all the things we've done together? We know each other so well, Joel—what could go wrong?"

"You are used to having me underfoot," Joel said lightly, to cheer away the unhappy frown on her usually open and candid face, and because he too wanted to savor these few last moments of love with her, uncomplicated by problems of the future. Somehow they would work out. "I may be gone for a very long time, and you will get used to being without me," he said. He swung her to face him with his hands hard on her shoulders. "Don't get used to being without me, Abby!" he said fiercely. "If it weren't for this war we must fight, it would be my desire to be with you now and for always."

She clung to him for a moment, then drew herself up proudly. "We *shall* be together always—I will marry you someday no matter what anyone says!"

He kissed her. "Good-by, dearest Abigail."

He walked off down the road with her words, in her high clear voice, echoing in his heart. He did not look round to see if she was watching him go; he knew that the sight of her would make him turn back for another, more painful good-by. He did not know what the months ahead had in store for him: misery, battle, killings—all the wasteful things, the things he hated. God had created human beings to love one another, to be fruitful, and contented—not to quarrel and make war. At the end of the road which lay ahead of him, God willing, there would be victory and peace and Abigail. *If* God is willing, he could not help thinking, and he sighed. Absolute faith was not for him, nor could he always understand the ways of God; he could only do the best he could to gain the things he wanted and believed in.

12.

December, 1778

THE shivering soldiers in the camp on Redding Ridge thought themselves forgotten men. The huts they had built were half-buried in snow; even the high wooded slope at the back did not protect the crude shelters from the bitter wind, or keep the wet flakes from whisking through cracks in the log walls. At the end of a woodland alley which was the Company Street, the Little River was frozen solid; holes made to fill kettles clogged almost instantly again with icy film.

Breakfast had been flour and water baked over the fire into hard biscuits which sat on Joel's stomach like thick pasteboard. The men in the hut were huddled as close to the chimney as they could get without scorching their eyebrows. Though the drums of reveille had dragged them out as usual at dawn, even the sternest of officers found no chores for their men to do on a day like this.

Stephen Sturgis was trying to get warm by polishing vigorously at the rust on his musket barrel; Bart Mead was grumbling to himself in a voice croaking with the pain of an inflamed throat; Moses Jones, the freed Negro, had drawn his blanket up over his head and sat wrapped like a mummy, as he had sat all through the night, fearing to stretch out lest the part of him furthest from the fire should freeze as he slept. Denis Leary's blanket only covered him part way, for he had torn off strips to bind round the cracked shoes on his sore and swollen feet. Though he was in pain, he grinned at Joel; it was more like the grimace of a death's head.

Joel laid aside the letter he had been trying to write to Abby; it was hopeless. The ink froze and the quill fell from his numb fingers. His eyeballs burned from the smoke-filled air and the cold. What could he write her anyway but tales of chilblain and bellyache?

Abby's letters to him were in a packet under his ragged shirt. Having them there made a small patch of warmth to comfort him, though they were troubled letters. Her parents refused to discuss her marriage to Joel. But Abigail's love did not waver. Joel closed his smarting eyes and summoned up the memory of her as he had last seen her, a year ago, her bright head held high, her little face determined. Had it not been for the letters, he might have thought he had dreamed that she loved him.

The packet was small, for it had not been easy to find a way of sending letters or indeed to keep track of Joel in his army wanderings. He was no newcomer to hardship, for he had spent the previous winter at Valley Forge; then there had been unsuccessful campaigns in New Jersey and Rhode

Island, and in the fall, his regiment had been sent to watch over the ammunition magazines in Connecticut and the towns along the Sound. To his disappointment, his orders brought him no closer to the house at Compo than these winter quarters near Danbury, a good twenty miles from Fairfield. Abigail seemed as far away as ever.

At least it was a help when he rejoined the Connecticut brigades, to find Denis again; his cheerful spirit lifted Joel somewhat from the disappointment and despair into which he found himself sinking. Noble ideals and patriot sentiments were hard to remember here. The camp at Redding droned like a beehive with complaints. Complaints about the food, the bad pay, the lack of winter clothing. Over camp chores and sentinel duty, over useless marches and bivouacs in the rain without tents. When someone, of a dripping, dreary dawn would open his eyes to say, "Good morning, Brother Soldier; how are you?" Denis would answer, "All wet, I thank you; hoping you are the same." It was one of the stock camp jokes, which after a while grew tiresome.

Then winter fell, and with it the snow. The men had huts now, for a little shelter; they cooked their miserable meals, gathered brush for the fires, made cartridges while there was powder and lead to make them with, cleaned their firelocks if they were not too careless even for that. Having nothing better to do they argued. Having no enemy to fight, they fought with one another.

Bart Mead's particular hate was for officers. He did not see why he should be called to wait on them. "Why should I salute some idjit because somehow he's got himself made a captain? I don't regard officers no more than broomsticks!"

126

"You wouldn't say that about the General, would you?" asked Stephen Sturgis, who was young and earnest and a bit better educated than Bart.

"Old Put is a smart farmer, and he's a smart general," Bart said. "Brave as a bull he is; a good hearty fellow. It's them young lieutenants that strut about like boar-pigs with their tails cut off."

This cold December day, the soldiers at Redding were more disgruntled than ever. When the ox teams that ordinarily brought their rations had not appeared by noon, the men began to pop their heads out of their huts, cawing like crows, hooting like owls, yelling, "No bread, no soldier!"

Denis, ever curious, cupped his hand around his ear. "If I can walk on these poor clods of mine, I'm going to see the fun. Come along, Joe?"

All of them decided it was time to stretch. On the Company Street, the men were standing round cook fires where there was not even the usual dried peas and salt meat to cook, scowling and grumbling of their injustices.

"Those fellows is going to get in a mighty lot of trouble if'n they keeps on yelling," Moses Jones said.

A man with a yellow face and a lantern jaw covered with a scrub of beard, turned to stare. He was so tall that he stood out among his fellows; also he was better clothed than most.

"Wonder where he got them good leather breeches," Bart Mead muttered. "Must've stole or cheated for 'em, 'cause they sure cost more than what we get paid."

Joel recognized the man as Alf Hodges, Squire Bailie's discharged farm hand, whom he had first seen at New London, tormenting the old Tory. Hodges looked at the Negro with distaste. "When they let niggers be soldiers, I reckon I've had enough of this army!" he remarked in a loud voice.

Joel was fond of Moses, who was an uncomplaining comrade and a good soldier, worth ten of Alf Hodges. As always, when angry, the Polish idiom returned to his speech. "And for why shouldn't they be soldiers?" he said. "Aren't they men like us, to fight for their human rights?"

Hodges walked over to Joel and looked him up and down. His lip drew back, showing the discolored teeth. "I remember you—the furriner. Of course I'd expect a feller like you to stand up for a nigger; you ain't exactly a white man yourself."

Joel was, for the moment, too angry to answer. This was the kind of man who went to war because he enjoyed the cruelty of it, the kind who delighted in tormenting those weaker than himself. Negroes, Jews, those who were politically unpopular like the old Tory in New London—all were fair game for Alf Hodges.

A crowd was gathering at the prospect of a fight. Joel wondered how many of them agreed with the bully, how many sneered at a Jew behind his back. Well, he might be the only Jew in this camp, but he did not feel weak and he was not going to back down. He took a step closer and said, "By God, Hodges, if all white men were like you, I wouldn't admit to being one!"

Denis came to Joel's side. "And if there's any of you that go along with that scum, speak up so I can take the hide off of him!"

Moses Jones plucked at Joel's sleeve. "Don't get into no trouble on account of me!"

128

"Hush up, Moses!" Joel snapped. "It is my fight, not yours. And mine alone," he said to Denis.

"Then let him have it, Red!" Denis cried. "I'll be right here behind you."

Joel flung the blanket from his shoulders and squared off. He knew little of fisticuffs but he was beyond caring whether he had skill or not. He plunged in and received a blow in the face that set him back on his heels. Impatiently he brushed away the blood that dripped from a cut cheek, not even feeling the smart of it, looking for a chance to land a punch of his own. Hodges, with a grin on his face, came toward him with thumbs extended. Joel knew what that meant—gouging, a nasty trick which toughs and frontiersmen considered fair fighting. He put up an arm to protect his eyes and Hodges punched him in the belly. Gasping, Joel flung himself on his enemy, holding himself up by hugging him like a bear. Hodges jerked a hand free, reached for his belt.

"Watch out, Joe; he's got a knife!" Denis squeaked.

Hearing the warning through ringing ears, Joel grabbed the man's wrist just in time. But he could not stop the blade from approaching. He watched it come, felt his own arm slowly, relentlessly bent backward. The knife point pricked against his breast through jacket and shirt. This is the end, Joel thought.

"Down on your knees and cry mercy, Jew!" Alf Hodges jeered.

Joel could only shake his head. He had neither time nor breath left to recite, "Hear, O Israel: the Lord our God, the Lord is One," as a good Jew should when death was near.

He needed each last bit of strength to push back the hand holding the knife.

"Stop them—it's no fair fight!" Denis shouted, forcing himself between them, and others jumped on Hodges, took the knife from his grip, and dragged him away. "He'd ought to be whipped and drummed out o' camp!" said one of the men as Hodges, cursing and struggling, was marched off. Denis and Stephen Sturgis hustled Joel into the hut and held him down till he stopped trying to lay about him as if he would fight them all.

"Too bad, old rooster," Denis said, clapping him on the shoulder. "That raccoon's a big fistful for either one of us, but the two of us could've waxed him good. Only you *would* want all the glory of licking him for yourself. Maybe this'll teach you to share things with your friend Denis."

Joel was not amused by Denis's teasing. He was disgusted that such a man as Hodges should be part of the same army as himself. He was disgusted and discouraged about everything. He sat glowering into the fire.

Outside the hut those who had gathered to see the fight went on to debating the old subject, their grievances. The blustering wind tossed the voices against the hillside to echo back. More men came to stew and seethe around the campfire. One of the number climbed astride a cannon and harangued the rest, pounding a mittened hand against the other. His fingers showed blue-cold through the holes in the worn mittens. The men listened, nodding approval, paying no attention to the snow that blew from overburdened pine branches into their raw red faces. "No pay, no soldier!" the man on the gun barrel was shouting. "We be going to get what's coming to us, by Glory!"

"Them miserable Congressmen in Philadelphy be drinking up all our pay," a man said. But Philadelphia was too far away to go with their demands. Hartford, the state capital, was closer.

At this idea, the men cheered, and several broke away and ran to rouse their fellows from the huts. One entered the cabin where Joel sat with his head in his hands, not even looking up when the open door made the smoke and sparks swirl from the fireplace. Bart Mead growled, "Come to wish us a happy New Year, Corporal? Where's our extra tot o' rum?"

"It ain't New Year yet," the corporal said.

"Why don't the General leave us go home for the holiday?" Bart groaned. "What's he keeping us here to freeze for?"

"I could stand for it, if only we were paid proper," Stephen Sturgis said.

"You don't figure us to be the best-paid army in the world then?" the corporal said cagily, looking from face to face to see how they took it.

Joel was off in his own thoughts; Moses had his blanket over his head again. Bart Mead blew through his nose. "Forty shillings a month sounds good till you try to buy something with the worthless paper. Look at this thing that's supposed to be a uniform!" He opened his blanket on a coat of tow cloth and breeches held together by strings. "I had to sell my buttons to get the necessaries."

"Such as grog?" said the corporal unsympathetically.

"I'd like to tell you grog is a necessary in climate like this," Bart said.

"Bart can make do without buttons if he wants to," said

131

Stephen Sturgis, "but to know your wife is starving on your pay is no joke."

"I heard tell Mr. Salomon was raising sound money to pay us with," Denis remarked.

"And I'll wager the Jew is making a pretty penny out of it for himself," Bart groused. Seeing Joel flush with anger, he added hastily, "I didn't mean you, Joe. I reckon I'm so peaked and cold these days I don't half know what I'm saying."

"Then keep your mouth shut!" Joel snapped.

"And don't let *me* hear you say anything against Mr. Salomon!" Denis said. "He risked his neck to shelter me, that wasn't one of his own, and that he'd never laid eyes on before. And who is it, Bart, I'd like to know, that sells the army those biscuits we call candle-bottoms, they're so bad? Yankee storekeepers, that's who."

"There are always cheats among every people," Joel said. "Let us forget it, Denis."

Stephen Sturgis, scratching himself busily, for he had the ground itch which came from sleeping on the earth, said, "I don't understand why Old Put don't look out better for us."

"Every man's got to look out for himself," Bart Mead said. "That's only common sense."

Maybe he's right, Joel thought. If the leaders of this revolution, Congress and the generals, didn't look out for them, why should the soldiers like himself bear the brunt of it?

"We just been talking over what could be done," the corporal said. "Come on outside, fellows, and hear about it."

"I don't want no trouble," Moses said, refusing to budge from his chimney corner. Denis took Joel's arm and dragged him along with the others. The plan, they learned, was for the brigades to march to Hartford where the Connecticut Assembly was in session, and there to demand that they be paid promptly in hard money.

"A sensible notion," said Denis, hugging himself. "I'm for it, if my feet will take me that far. What say, Joe?"

"It is mutiny," said Joel indifferently. "Well, why not?"

The men were swarming from the huts; soon the Company Street was packed solid. The air was frosty with brave talk: they'd throw a scare into the no-good politicians! They'd tell Brother Jonathan, the Governor, that they couldn't be made fools of! They dropped their blankets, picked up muskets, and formed into lines for a march on the state capital.

It was a relief to be doing something, anything; to be stamping life back into numb feet at least. But Joel's mind seemed to have gone numb as well. He no longer cared what happened. This was the way most revolutions ended, he thought. The faces of the men marching beside him, gaunt with hunger and red-blotched with frostbite, were bitter and hopeless. Their uniforms were any old things: homespun jackets of dingy green and mud-color, long loose hunting shirts, baggy pantaloons, rags round their legs to imitate leggings. Some had bound up their ears with strips of brown tow cloth. Gone were the jaunty feathers in their hats that had inspired the words of "Yankee Doodle Dandy." They had not joined up for the money there was in this army, but no cause could expect so much sacrifice for so long. And yet, they were ashamed of what they were doing this day; they were sullen, and they shuffled rather than marched.

The ring of a horse's hoofs sounded on the frozen road,

133

distant but coming fast. Word of the mutiny had reached General Putnam and just as the brigades were turning out from the camp grounds, he galloped up, his gray hair bristling, his ugly old face brick red. "Halt!" he bellowed.

And "Halt!" shouted the mutiny's own leaders, giving, in honor of Old Put, the order to present arms. The drummer boys rolled out a tattoo, and the men stood at attention to hear what their general had to say.

"My brave lads, whither are you going?" Putnam shouted. "Do you intend to invite the enemy to follow you into the country? Whose cause have you been fighting and suffering in: is it not your own?"

He scolded them like an angry father. "Don't you consider how much the country is distressed by the war and that your officers have not been better paid than yourselves?"

He rode down the line, staring hard into each face. The soldiers hitched uneasily, blinked, and tried to avoid meeting those keen old eyes. Joel wished he had stayed quietly in the hut with Moses.

Putnam's voice took on a confident ring. "We expect better times, and that the country will do us ample justice. Let us stand by one another, then, and fight it out like brave soldiers. Think what a shame it would be for Connecticut men to run away from their officers!"

The men stood rigid and silent, breathing a pattern of vapor on the cold air. And as Old Put rode slowly down the line once more, they snapped into a military salute; the drummer boys whirled their sticks and beat upon their drums. The brigade major leaped to the forefront of the ranks. "Shoulder—hoo!" he shouted. Without exception, muskets rattled smartly into place. The men wheeled like the King's own Grenadiers on parade and marched back to the Company Street, where they stacked their arms and dispersed to the huts.

Even Bart Mead conceded that they couldn't walk out on Old Put. "I reckon we're all in this war together."

It would be good to believe this, Joel thought, but it didn't seem to be true. Yankees were always picking fights with Southerners; Pennsylvanians hated Yorkers. Men like Bart Mead, who accepted him as a comrade, clung to their suspicions of Jews they did not know. Why then was he fighting this war, Joel asked himself. Because the cause was too great to be destroyed by prejudice and petty differences. He wasn't fighting just so Jews could have a home. "Oh ye who love *mankind*, stand forth!"

But, for the sake of winning, did you have to put up with those who didn't have the slightest idea what the war was about? These were the times that tried men's souls, Tom Paine had written. Joel's soul was sorely tried when he was made to feel the stranger, the ever wandering Jew. Well, he wasn't going to put up with Alf Hodges—as soon as he got another chance, he'd knock the stuffing out of him even if it meant taking a cruel beating himself.

But later in the day he heard that Hodges had vanished—deserted to the Tory side, the men thought, from the way he had been talking. He wasn't going to stick with an army full of niggers and Jews, and which had no chance of winning anyway, Hodges had said.

135

13.

1779

WINTER ended at last; spring came, and the Connecticut brigades marched back to guard the Hudson River Valley. Joel had been in the Army again for a year and a half now, and at the beginning of July he was made a corporal and was granted a brief furlough.

It was slow traveling through the wild country of Westchester, and by the time he and the army teamster with whom he was riding reached the outskirts of Fairfield, night had fallen. Eager as he was to see Abby, Joel did not know what sort of a welcome he would receive from the elder Bailies if he arrived unannounced at this hour. He rode on, thinking he would spend the night with Matt Barry in neighboring Black Rock.

The graceful white mansions of the gentry in Fairfield Center were shuttered and blind-looking in the deep shadow of thick foliage, dusty and smelling of midsummer. Here and there a crack of light showed through a shutter, but the streets were deserted. "Mighty strange there's no one about," the teamster remarked. " 'Pears like folks must've been told to stay indoors."

When Joel pounded on the door of Matt Barry's lodging, it was several moments before the captain, lantern in hand, opened it a cautious crack. "Well, Joel lad," he cried. "You're a sight that's good to see! Ain't brought a brigade o' regulars with you, by any chance?"

"What's up?" Joel asked.

"Ain't you heard the news o' New Haven?"

"*New Haven*? No, what? Tell me quickly!"

"Tryon, the Big Wolf, come there yesterday," Barry said. "Looted the whole town and burned a part of it. The college boys put up a good fight, and by morning, so many militia was gathered, Tryon took ship again."

"This worries me for the safety of my family," Joel said anxiously. He could not bear to think of little Zipporah at the mercy of Tryon's Hessian soldiers.

"Most likely they took to the hills, like all the townspeople that had any sense. Only the Tories stayed, on account of Tryon promised they'd be safe. But your brother-in-law ain't no Tory, and he knows too much to trust Tryon's promises anyway."

"I hope so," Joel said.

"Now the point is, where's the Wolf going next? We figure he's gobbled down enough for now, but we been keeping watch just the same."

"Suppose he comes here?"

Matt shrugged. "There's not much we can do to get ready;

137

mighty few men of fighting age left in Fairfield. Lieutenant Jarvis has twenty-three at the fort on Grover's Hill, and there's a handful of us old militia men. The Coast Guard'll warn us if we're needed."

"Suppose Tryon should go to Compo, like he did in '77?"

"I know what you're worried over," Matt Barry winked. "I heard you was sparking little Abigail. But them few houses in the West Parish ain't worth the attention of a big squadron like this is said to be. If Tryon comes at all, it'll be after the flour mills here in Black Rock, and the rich houses on the Green at the Center. We might as well bed down for the rest of the night and get some rest while we can."

July 7th: still dark; the breath of dawn touched the sleepers in hot bedchambers under the low pitched roofs of Fairfield, and a promise of sunrise silhouetted the eastern shore. A cock crowed; at Black Rock, the cannon in the fort boomed.

Joel, asleep in the first real bed he had known in months, stirred and groaned. Now, as the fort gun boomed again, he sprang up, suddenly wide awake. Grabbing their muskets, Matt and he hurried to Grover's Hill.

There was no real sunrise, only a hazy glow in the east, and daylight spreading slowly overhead. Far out on the Sound a phantom squadron was drifting westward in the direction of New York. The sun dodged out of the mist like a pale penny and vanished again as the thickening fog rolled down to hide everything but a few yards of gray water lapping on the beach.

"Do you think they'll come back?" Joel asked.

"Mebbe."

"I'm going to Compo."

Matt held his arm. "No, you don't. Your Abigail is safe enough; all the women been warned to take to the hills if Tryon comes. You stay here—we need every able-bodied man we can get; there's so pitifully few of us."

"I suppose you are right."

They sat on the hill above the fort, with their guns across their knees, staring into the billowing fog that lifted and settled and lifted again, revealing now the rocks of Penfield Reef; now a small boat at anchor; now the tasseled hummocks of Fayerweather Island. By mid-morning, watery sunlight began to glimmer on the ripples, and on boat-loads of marines, rowing in toward the mill wharves at the foot of the very hill where they sat. And beyond, off the point, the whole fleet was coming to anchor: men-of-war, row galleys, and transports—more than a score of them.

The fort guns pounded the invaders, but when the smoke of the explosions lifted, the boats were still crawling through the haze, waving their hundred oars. A few minutes later, tongues of fire shot up from the bakehouse on the creek, while, raked by the fire from the fort, the marines retreated to their ships, out of range. They had accomplished their mission; for many months to come, Washington's hungry army would receive no flour from Penfield Mills, or loaves of bread from Black Rock.

Matt Barry jumped up. "They'll be landing most likely on the beach where the fort guns can't reach them. Come on, Joel."

But there were creeks to cross and quagmires to skirt in order to reach the lane leading to the beach. Long before the two men got there, they could hear musket fire and the roar of a small fieldpiece on the Court House Green at Fairfield. The enemy had already landed three divisions, and the militia men, having held them off as long as they could, were retreating to the hills which overlooked the town. Matt Barry and Joel fell into step with them. On the slope of Round Hill they all sat down, to watch and wait for reinforcements.

A youngster, fingering his flintlock, eyed Joel's badge of rank, and edged closer in the grass. "You be a veteran," he said timidly.

"Here and there I have been in the Army some time, but I have not fought enough to be proud of it," Joel said kindly, touched by the boy's face, so like Abner Bailie's, and his blond hair lank with the sweat of fear.

"We been drilling," the boy said, "and I shoot pretty good at rabbits and such. But I never yet stood up to be shot at." He yawned. "I can't figure why I do that. I ain't drowsy—I must be woefully scared!"

Joel smiled and put his hand for a moment on the boy's rigid shoulder. "You are plagued with gaping, and I'm a little sick at the belly each time I face the enemy. Waiting is the worst part. When they come, you'll be all right."

"Will you stick by and tell me when I do right and when I do wrong?"

"If you wish it."

They lay there on the slope of the hill, clutching their muskets in damp hands. The meadow grass pricked them; insects droned; ants crawled over them and mosquitoes stung. Looking down, they saw the thick foliage of the elms around

140

the Green, with here and there a glimpse of brown roof or white church tower. Half hidden by the trees, red soldiers strutted through the streets; bugles tootled with a gay scornful note, and Hessian officers barked commands. Beyond the town they could see the salt meadows stretching to the Sound shimmering in a heat haze.

The commandant asked for thirty volunteers for a scouting party. Instantly, a hundred crowded around him, clamoring to go. "I compliment you on your courage," he said, "but so large a force could not make a foray undetected. Captain Nash, you will lead, and I will pick the most experienced to support you. Matthew Barry—and you, sir," he pointed to Joel and went on down the line, selecting those he knew or those who seemed most calm and sure. He passed over the youngster at Joel's side.

They had been waiting on the hilltop all afternoon, and now the sun was slanting behind the western slopes, casting long shadows over the town. Evening mists were beginning to rise from the marshes.

"You have each your gill cupful of powder and fifteen balls, or a like amount in cartridges?" Captain Nash asked his company. "Very well then, follow me."

They began the descent, crouching low over their firearms. Joel felt a shy touch on his shoulder. It was the boy. Like many others he had joined the party as soon as the commandant's back was turned. Joel grinned at him reassuringly. They crept through the fields, crushing the black-eyed Susans that were orange gold in the sunset light, catching their breeches on thorns of blackberry vine and wild rose. Whenever they dared, they would make a dash across the open and fling themselves down again behind a boulder or bush, watching to see that the coast was clear and that no sentries had spied them before scrambling to the next bit of shelter. Each yard closer to the town was closer to danger; each minute Joel expected they would be welcomed with a shower of bullets.

But Tryon had posted no watchdogs; and the Hessian officers were letting their men rampage through the town at will, helping themselves as was their custom. The Minute Men crept to the very edge of a street and hid in tall weeds behind a fence. "When I give the word," Captain Nash whispered, "fire; load and fire once again, and then run for it."

Joel bit off the end of a cartridge case and loaded his gun. "Poise your firelocks," whispered Captain Nash. A foraging party was coming down the street, headed by a jaunty young officer swinging his sword lightly in his gloved hand. The company had a devil-may-care look, quite different from that of the well-disciplined British Regulars; their uniform was different too. Their hats sat rakishly on their unpowdered heads and their buttons were unpolished. It was a company of come-lately Tories, renegades who had deserted from the Continental Army.

"Take aim—fire!" ordered Captain Nash.

The British officer fell headlong, and as his men ran to help him, others fell, wounded by the second round. The Americans made for the hills, losing themselves in the twilight.

Only one Minute Man lagged behind, turning, contrary to

142

orders, to fire a third round. A blast of musketry answered him, and he pitched forward on his face.

In the last bit of light lingering at the top of the hill, Joel walked among the men who sprawled on the grass, looking for the boy he had befriended. He alone was missing; he was the one who had lingered and fallen. He had not lived even long enough to know he was no coward, to enjoy boasting perhaps a little. People might say he was a brave lad, and for a while they would speak of it, but he would never hear them, and it would be small comfort to his mother and father, whoever they might be. Somehow it seemed more pitiful for the boy to fall in this very first encounter than if he had lived a little while before being killed. But in the eyes of history it made no difference.

Lights were beginning to wink in the trees around the Green. They grew stronger, too fierce and bright for candle flames. Leaves crisped and whirled away in a welter of dancing red sparks. Matt Barry stared. "They've fired the Jennings house."

All through the town, the flames were breaking out now, creeping and joining together, till the fire roared like a hearth blaze leaping at the breath of a bellows. But no wind stirred; it was sulphurously hot and smothering to the lungs. The smoke hung leadenly above the burning houses, reflecting the bloody glare. Overhead, storm clouds were piling up and lightning forked across the horizon.

"God is sending the tempest to save our homes," one of the men said prayerfully.

"It will take more than a summer storm to quench this hellfire," Matt Barry answered.

143

The gale gusted suddenly out of the south, fanning the flames to even greater fury. The ominous clouds split with blinding light. Thunderclap after thunderclap rolled across the water like the broadsides of some mighty ship of the line. Joel felt the ground shake under him and when he closed his eyes against the flashes, the lurid red light came through his eyelids. In pauses between thunderclaps, you could hear the loud crackling of the flames and the thudding of the guns as the row galleys attacked the little fort at Black Rock, and the fort answered them.

All night long the Minute Men lay on the hilltop watching, and every hour more men came through tangled pathways, woods and swamps from neighboring towns to join them. The rain fell, and they lay on their firelocks to keep them dry. The sprinkling passed, and the flames still licked; the air was hot and oppressive as ever. In the grass an insect army chanted monotonously, paying no heed to the armies of men.

Below, in the town, a rooftree crashed and a fountain of sparks gushed up. "There goes everything I own," a man said bitterly.

"There goes the best early crop we've had since the war started," Matt Barry said, as the ring of fire widened, spreading to outlying barns and haymows.

The thunder rolled away into the distance; the storm had passed, but a hideous racket took its place: wild shouts, hoots and catcalls. "It could be a witches' Sabbath," Joel said. "Is this the English gentlemen's idea of how one makes war?"

"I reckon Tryon figures if things get bad enough, us Connecticut folk will yell to Washington that he should send the Army here to protect us. That would leave the Hudson Valley hard-up for soldiers."

A woman's scream rose above the drunken laughter.

Joel rolled over in the grass and put his lips to Matt Barry's ear. "How long do we wait before we silence those devils?"

"Till the colonel thinks there's enough of us to chance it."

"I'm sick of waiting," Joel said, inching away. "I shall have a look below; they are too full of wine to know who comes."

"I'm with you," Matt said.

They crawled on their bellies till they were so close that the smoke smarted their eyes. Close enough to hear the splintering of wood, the crash of glass and crockery; to see against the glare, burly shapes that prodded with bayonets, clubbed with gun butts. An infant wailed pitifully, and then was suddenly still. Like an avenging prophet, Joel began to babble Hebrew: " 'They know not what they do . . . who store up violence and robbery in their palaces!' "

"Quit your gibberish!" Matt Barry croaked. "Do you want the Hessians to get us?"

From behind a smoking pile that had been a graceful white church, a company of Germans came reeling and singing. They had rings on their fingers and bracelets on their wrists that sparkled, in the light of the fires, ruby red. They dangled strings of copper pots and gaily beat time with silver spoons on silver teakettles. Silk shawls draped their shoulders and one, with a woman's plumed hat crooked on his head, was caroling drunkenly:

"Shtuck a fedder in his hat
Und callt it Macaroni! "

Joel started up, but Matt Barry pressed him to earth with his sinewy arms. "Be still, you fool!"

"They are too drunk to know what they do," Joel whispered. "Now we could jump the foul-mouthed, dirty animals!"

"Not those fellows, Red—those are Yaegers. They fight like Injuns, drunk or sober. And there's twenty of 'em to two of us."

Thwarted, more impatient than ever, Joel watched the Yaegers carom down the street.

"Ain't you learned yet that it's no part of a soldier's job to throw his life away useless—like that boy did on the foray?" Barry asked.

Joel's eye blazed at him. "You don't know the language. If you understood what the pigs were saying, as I did. . . ."

"What did they say?"

"That the *verdamte Amerikaner* were all cowards that ran to the hills and left their women to defend the town. And they laughed particularly because of one woman who said Tryon had promised her protection—so they took her valuables, half-pulled her clothes off, and burned her house down. She was old and ugly, they said, or they would have had more fun with her."

But Abigail was not old and ugly. "I am going to Compo," Joel said, getting to his feet. "This time you won't persuade me from it."

It was growing light, though the pall of smoke veiled the feeble sunrise. A dying bonfire lay before them, a mass of smoldering ruins, charred beams at crazy angles, tall blackened chimneys rising from red embers. From the edges of the ash heap, new fires were still spreading.

"It's morning; soon there'll be action," Matt Barry said. "Wait, Joel; we need you."

"Not so much as I may be needed elsewhere," Joel said. "I'll see you later, Matt."

14.

JOEL came up over the brow of Compo Hill and flattened himself among the grasses. From this high place he should be able to see whatever was going on in the neighborhood. At his right hand, wooded slopes and pastures curved peacefully away into milky distances; on his left a thunderhead of smoke hung over plundered Fairfield. Beyond was the wide basin of the Sound, riffling blue in the morning breeze, creaming in bright ripples on the yellow beaches. And directly below, rocking gently in the mouth of the Saugatuck, were two British row galleys.

It was no longer a time for cautious slow approach. He pelted down the slope, scrambling over stone walls, lurching into hidden holes. Once he rolled part of the way, but grimly kept hold of his musket. Only as he came very near to the Bailie house and saw smoke rising from the chimney, did he take cover behind scattered cedars. One of the shuttered windows was open and the odor of roasted meat and freshly baked Indian-meal muffins made his empty stomach grumble. Everything looked and smelled like breakfast time on any normal day; was it possible that the family was totally ignorant of the enemy boats at anchor close by? Some inner sense made him stop to listen carefully before walking boldly to knock at the door. There was nothing to hear but the usual barnyard sounds: a hen announcing the triumph of an egg; the cow complaining because she had not yet been let out to pasture. No sign of red coats, the Hessian uniforms of blue and white, or the green and scarlet of the Chasseurs, in garden, field or orchard.

He stepped from behind his screen of bushes, advanced a few paces, and had to fling himself down between the rows of bean poles in the kitchen garden to avoid being seen by a Yaeger who scurried off on the road to the beach, chuckling to himself in high good humor. When the German had disappeared, Joel ran to the front of the house. Another Yaeger was pacing up and down before the doorstep. Joel took aim with his gun.

Slowly he lowered it again. He could hear a man's voice in the house, a rough and demanding voice, not Gurdon's or Squire Bailie's. There might be more than one enemy inside; there might be too many for him, and a shot would bring them swarming. When the sentry passed close to his hiding place, Joel leaped out and brought the stock of his musket down on the fellow's head. He crumpled up with a low grunt of pain. He was just a boy, Joel saw, a raw country lad, with beardless apple cheeks, who looked no more capable of brutality than Gurdon. One of the hundreds of innocent peasant boys whom the lords of Hesse-Cassel pressed into service against their will, no doubt. Joel, glad to find him still breathing in spite of the rising lump on his skull, dragged the limp body behind the cedar clump, and ran to look in at the window, crouching low so as not to be seen himself from inside.

He hoped that the family had fled to the hills, and that he would spy no one inside but a company of soldiers. Instead he saw Abigail. Though she stood straight and defiant, either fear or anger was making her starched cap and apron shake like leaves in a wind. Facing her, a man in Tory uniform was comfortably sprawled at the kitchen table where a tankard of ale, a roast joint, and a trencher piled with delicacies was set before him. It was Alf Hodges, coat unbuttoned over a dirty shirt, long legs spread wide, playing with a pistol in one hand, stuffing food into his mouth with the other.

Again Joel raised his musket to shoot. But Abigail was directly in the line of fire.

"All you folks used to think I was dirt, didn't you?" Alf Hodges said. "Your pa spoke big about the rights of man— but treat me like an equal? Not him!"

"My father treated you kindly and paid you what you earned," Abigail said. "He turned you out because you were a lazy, thieving rascal!"

"Lazy, is it? Thief, is it? I knew some day I'd show you I was as good as you—if not in one army, then in the other. So now *I'm* cock o' the roost here and you can wait on *me*, Missy!" He shoved the flagon at her. "Fetch me more ale from the cellar and be quick about it."

Abigail knocked the flagon from his hand. "I've waited

on you enough," she said. "You've had your breakfast; now go away and leave us in peace!"

Alf Hodges jumped up and twisted her arm behind her back. "You do what I say!" he bellowed. Abigail turned white and caught her lip with her teeth to keep from crying out.

Joel vaulted the sill and flung himself on the pair with a blow that made Hodges loose his grip. He glared at Joel, recognition flickering across his face for a moment before Joel sent the pistol spinning and they locked arms. Hodges was foggy with drink, while Joel had grown tough and wiry from months of soldiering. They were no longer so unevenly matched, and rage gave Joel added strength. His hands gripped the fellow's throat; Hodges went limp, and his bulging eyes begged for mercy. A wave of revulsion swept Joel at the cringing terror in those eyes; he loosened his grip.

Abigail had picked up the pistol and was pointing it at Hodges, who, feeling painfully of his throat, croaked out, "I didn't mean nothing. I was just being friendly, that's all. I come here to protect the young lady from them Yaegers."

"The lady can do without your friendship and protection," Joel said. "Give me the pistol, Abigail."

"You—you wouldn't shoot an old comrade, would you?" the man cried.

"You were never my comrade," Joel said. "But Americans don't shoot unarmed prisoners."

Hodges saw that soft words would get him nowhere. "Americans!" he spat out. "I done right to change sides. Niggers, Jewish swine, *anything* can call himself American!"

"Quite true. Anyone can call himself American who knows

what it means. Naturally you are *not* one; you are garbage. Garbage too filthy even for this Jewish swine. Abigail, fetch a rope, will you?"

Hodges, tied up, regarded them both, red-eyed. "You won't have your fun for long. I been scouting for the Yaegers—the rest of them'll be up from the boats any minute."

"Many thanks for warning me," Joel said.

With Joel's arms around her, Abigail at last relaxed and wept a little. "My father and Gurdon went off to join the Minute Men, thinking the enemy would not come here. Oh Joel, if it had not been for you, what would have happened to us?"

He kissed her, but he said, "We must leave immediately, my dear one. I am not enough to hold off an army."

"My mother!" Abigail cried. "She is bound and gagged, in the buttery."

Joel gave her his knife. "Hurry—we have little time."

Now it was Joel who tossed the pistol in his hand, regarding Alf Hodges thoughtfully. "Really, I should kill you before we go."

Again the man cringed as he realized the blunder he had made. "I'll tell the Yaegers to spare you all," he said cunningly. "You'll never get away otherwise, specially if you shoot me. You ain't got the time to get away—they'll be here any minute now."

"You will tell them to spare the house as well?" Joel asked.

"Of course!"

"You promise this?"

"On my honor."

152

Joel walked to the window and looked out; quickly pulled the shutters to and barred them, for already he had seen the gleam of bayonets in the distance; the grass plumes tossing and nodding as they were pushed aside by the Yaegers approaching from the shore. He turned back to stare at Hodges, whose shifty eyes blinked and dropped. "I have a good idea what your honor and your promises are worth," Joel said. "About as much as the promises of your General Tryon. I am not so big a fool as to rely on your word of honor." He interrupted the low voices in the next room. "Abigail!" he cried.

"In a moment, Joel. Mother is stiff and pained; the bonds were very tight."

"Come quickly, nevertheless."

She ran swiftly to him.

"You two must go out by a back window—now, right away," he said.

"You mean—they are coming. Then you must flee too, Joel."

"I'll stay here to hold them off for a little. I'll be safe enough inside the house."

"No." She planted her feet. "If you don't go, I will stay too."

"But Abby," he said impatiently, expecting any minute to hear the tramp of feet outside, "be reasonable; go—go now, or it will be too late. This fellow promises he will tell them to spare me."

"But you don't trust him—I heard you say so."

"If he breaks his word, I have always the pistol and the

musket," he said lightly enough. "These can take care of a good many Yaegers."

Abigail picked up the musket he had dropped on entering. "I know how to shoot too," she said.

"We New England women are not afraid of death, Joel," said Mistress Bailie from the doorway.

Hodges snorted. "Don't you all sound brave and noble, though! As if the Yaegers wouldn't dare touch such as you! Pretty soon you'll be humble enough, begging me for help!"

"Give me cloth for a gag, Abby," Joel said quietly. He stuffed it into the prisoner's mouth and bound a kerchief round. "I am tired of the sound of his voice."

In the long silence while they waited, the tiny sounds of the house grew big: the old floorboards creaking, squirrels scurrying across the roof, a cricket chirping gaily as if everything was normal as on any other day. And finally they heard the sound for which all four were listening.

Joel dropped to one knee by the window and sighted the pistol through the loophole in the shutter. Abigail took a position at another window.

15.

"*ACHTUNG—HALT!*"

The feet stopped; some of them still shuffling a little. Muskets were grounded with a thump. A man cleared his throat. Abigail was carefully pouring powder into the pan of her firearm as she had seen her father do. Joel motioned to her to wait; swiftly he went to the prisoner and pressed his pistol against Hodges' temple.

"You will tell them to go away," he whispered.

Hodges twisted in his bonds and his face grew purple. He was trying desperately to spit out the gag.

"If you do not do what I say, I will kill you," Joel said calmly. "Tell them to go away and not to come back for one hour. If we don't escape, I will have the pleasure of killing you first."

Hodges frowned and blinked; his pasty face turned green. There could be no doubt that Joel would do what he said. He bobbed his head.

"Take the gag out, Abby," Joel whispered, keeping his pistol hard against the man's forehead. "Now, you tell them!"

"Go away," said Hodges thickly.

"*Was ist das?*" The voice was puzzled, disgusted, unbelieving.

Joel poked with the pistol. "Louder, and as if you mean it. Remember I shoot otherwise."

"Go away, you dumb fools, and come back later; don't you understand?" Hodges shouted.

But still there was no sign of departure, and the mutters grew louder. The Yaegers did not see why they should take orders from this fellow Hodges. He had served his purpose as a guide, but that was all; he was no better than they were. The door shook, as one tried it with his shoulder. A musket stock crashed against it. Even the stout oaken panels would not stand this kind of treatment very long.

Hodges was sneering openly; in a moment he would grow bold enough to shout out the truth. Joel motioned to Abby to replace the gag. He would have to take a wild chance on a trick he had thought up; there was no longer anything to lose by trying it. For a moment he closed his eyes in order to think back to his childhood, to remember the German officers whom he had sometimes seen in Poland, to remember how they had sounded when they had been addressing the men under them.

He drew himself up, to play his part with proper arrogance. "*Schweinhunde!*" he shouted, and barked out an order in the men's own language, threatening them with flogging, imprisonment, even death, if they interfered further

156

with him and his Tory friend while they were enjoying their breakfast.

There was a sudden silence. Joel hardly dared to hope that he had succeeded—that the Yaegers would swallow this unexpected appearance of an unidentified *Oberleutnant* —one whose German was spoken with a Polish accent besides. But he had gambled correctly on their fears. There were anxious whispers, and the feet tramped off.

Joel made sure they had gone; then he and Abby and her mother quickly slipped out the back and hurried away, taking the path over the hill. When they had reached the top, Mistress Bailie turned for a last look at the house below. She put her hand to her breast as though wounded. "They have come back already," she said.

Joel did not need to ask how she knew. Thick smoke was rising from the hollow, above the plumed willows; a terrified squawking issued from the hen house; the cow was bawling. Abigail put her arms around her mother, whose face was a mask of pain. "Our house has stood against hurricane and flood and Indian raids," Mistress Bailie said. "Now it is gone forever. May God punish those who do this."

"Come, Mistress Bailie," Joel said gently, "we have no time to linger."

"You do not know," Abigail's mother said bitterly, "what it is to lose a home that has stood for a hundred years."

"No—only what it is to lose one's home many times."

"Forgive me, Joel," Mistress Bailie said humbly. "I did not think."

Patches of flame were scattered through all of the West Parish, they saw, as they trudged onward. The Green's

Farms Meeting House was a blazing torch among the trees. "We have worshiped there each Sabbath as long as I can remember," Abigail said to her mother. Mistress Bailie nodded with stony face.

They turned away from the coast and followed the small pathways made by the Indians long ago through woods and fields, coming on many friends and neighbors who had lost their homes. It was a weary way to travel till they reached the settlement at Greenfield Hill where houses were still standing and the refugees found shelter.

Joel left them there and returned to join the militia men who were milling around Fairfield Green. Tryon, as usual when the odds against him grew too great, had re-embarked and set sail across the Sound, apparently headed for the British base in Huntington. Next day Major Tallmadge arrived with a regiment of Continentals from White Plains to camp among the smoking ruins on the Green. Here was a chance for Joel to meet Nathan Hale's friend, but before he could do so, word came that Tryon had returned and was raiding Norwalk. Minute Men and Regulars set off on the double for the neighboring town, but again they were too late. Tryon had looted Norwalk and set fire to it, and once more departed.

By the time the militia reached there, the townspeople were already coming down from the hills to which they had fled, and were poking in the rubble of their homes to find a few things with which they could cover themselves, cook food, and start a new life. One woman was weeping over a scorched bundle of patchwork quilts she had spent years in stitching; another was joyfully clutching a silver ewer she had rescued from the well where she had hidden it. Joel wandered among the ruins, stopping here and there to help lift a heavy beam or dig a domestic treasure from under the collapsed walls where shattered glass and twisted copper sparkled like jewels amid the charred black wood. A fog of smoke still hung over the town, smelling of burned feathers and melted fat.

He saw many Jewish faces among the victims, for Norwalk was a center for those who had fled from the British occupation of New York. He came upon a young girl comforting two small children with an air of maternal compassion far beyond her years. She held on her arm a little girl of three, and one slightly older, with a moon face and dark curls like Zipporah, clung to her skirts. "There, there, Deborah," she was soothing the baby, "your mama and papa have gone to find us shelter. Hush, Sara—soon we will get something to eat, I know."

She looked up and saw Joel watching. In her pale and soot-grimed face, the violet eyes looked enormous and still frightened by what they had seen, but she smiled and stretched out a hand. "Joel Davidov!"

"Judith—it *is* Judith Levino?"

She flushed; her hand went to her thick, tumbled dark hair. "How I must look—no wonder you don't know me!" Both children began to howl at the sight of the battle-stained stranger with the gun, who, for all they knew, might be another of those wicked Hessians. He kneeled down and took small Sara's hand. "I won't hurt you, little one. I am a friend —Judith will tell you so."

The child stared at him, frowning and doubtful; pulled

away and began to comfort her rag puppet, telling *it* not to be afraid.

"How is it possible that you are here?" Joel asked Judith. "*Your* father wouldn't need to flee New York."

"My parents have gone to England," Judith said. "Rachel was always eager for it, and when David was sent there as a prisoner, after the fall of Fort Washington, my parents decided to go."

"Your brother is a prisoner of war? Have you heard anything from him?" Joel remembered the young man warmly, and hoped things were not too grim for him in prison.

"He has been paroled, and he is quite well. I suppose my whole family will remain there, at least till the war ends. If it ever does." She sighed.

"But you haven't explained how *you* came here, instead of going with your parents to England."

"I did not disobey them, I promise you," she said with a smile. "I only said to them that I could not, with conscience, leave my country to live in one which is my enemy. My mother understood, and she persuaded Papa to let me come here with my aunt and uncle, the parents of these poor babes." She smoothed the baby Deborah's tangled curls and kissed the tear-stained, grimy cheek. "Now," she said, leaning down to Sara, "you must tell our friend Joel that you trust him."

"Cousin Jo-el?" Sara asked gravely.

"Not all of our friends are our cousins," she corrected, and explained. "She has been kept at home very much and thinks everyone we know must naturally be family."

"I should be proud to have such patriot kin," Joel said, and added, to tease her, "Cousin Judith!"

"I must go," Judith said hastily. "We are expected at the home of a friend, which luckily is still standing."

Sara began to wail that she was tired; she wanted to be carried like Deborah. "Will you trust me now?" Joel asked her. The child nodded solemnly, and Joel swung her to his shoulder. He followed Judith as she picked her way among the ash heaps, awkward yet sturdy under the weight of the little one she carried so tenderly. She had a sweet disposition, young Judith, very different from her imperious sister. Very different too, from Abby's boylike directness and high spirits. Yet there must be inner fire here too; it had taken a strong will to stand up to her parents and courage to remain behind when they had gone across the sea.

Joel set little Sara down at the door of the house Judith indicated and said good-by. "Will you not wait to meet my uncle?" Judith said. "And our friends will wish to give you some refreshment, if Tryon has left anything at all in the larder."

Joel thanked her but said he could not stay. He was impatient to return to Abigail, for he had only a brief time to spend with her before he would have to depart for camp. His furlough time was over; he had only an hour in which to bid Abigail farewell and hope that their difficulties and the fortunes of war would not continue to keep them apart.

161

16.

1780

IT WAS well over a year before Joel saw Fairfield and Abigail again, a year of bad fortune for the Continental Army, of weariness and loss of hope among the people. The Southern colonies were being overrun by the enemy. In the Hudson River Valley, where Joel was stationed with the Connecticut brigades, another bitter winter added to the soldiers' discomfort.

Yet he himself was feeling more hopeful about events as his own fortunes took an up-swing. Now when the wind blew and the snow fell, the packet of letters from Abigail warmed him by their happy tone: her father, grateful to Joel, no longer raised objections to their betrothal. Joel must come soon, to seal it, she wrote plaintively, for she was going on nineteen; soon she would be an ancient maid.

"And if there is danger of it, my dear Abby," Joel wrote in reply, "it is not because of unwillingness on my part to alter your state."

162

In the spring, he was made a sergeant, and he was pleased with this reward for being a good soldier. He determined to ask for a transfer to Major Tallmadge's regiment; it might bring him closer to Fairfield. Benjamin Tallmadge was now in charge of the whaleboat men who conducted secret service missions across the Sound. Tory raids on Connecticut towns continued, though on a smaller scale, and Tallmadge had recently been given a special command for the purpose of knocking out the British garrisons which served as headquarters for the raiders. When Joel told him that he had gone on several expeditions to Long Island with Matt Barry, Tallmadge was delighted to have him join his detachment of dismounted dragoons. All summer they shuttled back and forth from Westchester to Connecticut, but never, to Joel's disgust, coming to Fairfield.

Now it was late November, and Sergeant Joel Davidov was riding at last toward the house at Compo. Major Tallmadge had conceived a bold scheme for an expedition, figuring that a crossing of the Sound so late in the season would be likely to take the British by surprise. Fifty men were picked to go to Fairfield for the embarkation, but when they reached the harbor, autumn gales were blowing, the Sound was whipped to a froth, and there was no chance that the whaleboats could cross safely in such seas. Tallmadge gave Joel permission to absent himself for some hours each day while they waited for the weather to clear.

The very trappings of his horse jingled merrily as he jogged over the familiar hills from Black Rock to the Saugatuck. The russet November colors were spiked by dark green cedars and laced with the silver gray of bare branches. Beyond the tawny marshes, the water was purple gray and white breakers boomed on the rocks as if it were the ocean. How beautiful Connecticut is, even at this dreary season, Joel thought, and his heart warmed as if he were really coming home. He kicked his horse into a canter down the lane toward the new house Squire Bailie had built on the foundations of the old one. It was hardly more than a cabin backed up against the tall blackened chimney. Abigail had been watching; the door flew open at the sound of the hoofbeats. Her slimness was more rounded; her fair curls were neatly combed beneath her cap, but Abby would not have been Abby without some trace of the former hoyden. Instead of walking sedately to greet him, as her mother would have wished, she picked up her gray merino skirts and ran headlong. Then, when he leaped from the saddle to embrace her, she half pulled away. "You are almost a stranger, Joel—you must ask my father's permission before you spark me," she said, half demure, half teasing. He felt a bit awkward himself; it was a year and a half since he had last seen Abby.

Squire Bailie greeted him with a return of the old hearty manner Joel had first known. "If it had not been for you, I should not now have a daughter whose hand I could bestow in marriage," he said. "We are lucky to have so courageous a young man as Abby's future spouse." Joel thanked him, but could not help thinking wryly that it had taken quite a bit of doing for him to be accepted as any decent Gentile suitor would have been.

But indeed both Abigail's parents were kind to the young couple, withdrawing to their own bedchamber so that the two could be alone together, since they had been so much apart. They were happy in growing to know one another again; they spent the evening hours by the fire telling each other of their love. Joel spoke of his ambition to be a schoolmaster when peace came—"Not a Rabbinical scholar searching for obscure meanings. I want to teach ordinary boys and girls what this country means, tell them of history, read to them from Tom Paine and Mr. Jefferson and the lessons of the Scriptures which are as true now as the day they were written." He smiled sheepishly. "When I get on this subject, I drone on like a bumblebee and waste our precious hours. You must forgive me, Abby."

"There is nothing to forgive," she said happily. "These are the things that I too believe."

Joel approached Squire Bailie on the subject of the betrothal. "I should like my nearest male relative, Jacob Peretz, to meet with you. Who knows when I will be able to come this way again?" Abigail's father agreed that the formalities should be discussed, and Joel's brother-in-law was sent for.

Jacob rode from New Haven a day later with his wife on the pillion behind him. When Joel lifted Miriam down, her eyes were brimming. "My little brother—Yosele the scholar —to be married soon. It hardly seems possible."

"I am twenty-two, Miriame," he said, squeezing her hand. It was cold and nervous, though she bore herself with dignity.

Abigail and Gurdon and their parents came out to greet them. "She is very pretty, your beloved," Miriam whispered in Yiddish. "I wish only that she was one of us, and not Gentile-born."

Though he had no time to answer her, Joel was shocked. He had not expected Miriam to express this attitude.

165

The Bailies were apologizing for their makeshift house, the few poor sticks of furniture, the vessels of iron and wood. "You do not need to do explaining, Mistress Bailie," Joel's sister said. "We also suffered from the raiders, though we were lucky; we did not lose the home itself this time."

The table was spread with a new linen cloth, with ale and cider and cakes and honey; Mistress Bailie had been at pains not to offer any food that might insult her guests. Under her austere Puritan manner, Joel knew, there was a kind heart and a brave soul. Proudly he watched Abigail seated at the other end of the table with her small hands clasped on the starched white apron that covered the blue wool of her skirt. Her cheeks were very pink, her eyes downcast save when she raised them to smile at him, and then it was like spring suddenly blossoming. He felt that he had never been so happy, surrounded by all those whom he loved best in the world. All but little Zipporah; Miriam had said she was too young to bring.

When the women had removed themselves to the other chamber, the men settled down to discuss the business before them. "The laws of the Connecticut Commonwealth are founded on the ancient code of Moses, and must therefore be familiar to you," Squire Bailie said to Jacob. "The pre-contract must be publicly posted for eight days, and after that another eight days must go by before the betrothal covenant is signed."

Jacob nodded. "Then Joel—may the Lord keep him with us till then—gives your daughter the betrothal ring, which consecrates her to him. Let us discuss the contract."

For his part, Squire Bailie said, he would give Abigail as

fair a marriage portion as he could afford in these trouble-some times. Jacob replied that he was sure Joel would not want to higgle over the dowry.

"I cannot promise to endow Abigail with much of worldly goods," Joel said. "School teaching does not give a very rich living. But I promise to take care of Abigail tenderly always, and see to her comfort."

"It will suffice." Squire Bailie rose and shook hands with Jacob. "I will see to the drawing up of the papers."

When his kinsfolk had departed, Joel dropped the digni-fied air of the prospective bridegroom. He seized Abby by the waist and swung her into the air, as dizzy and gay as if he had drunk off a beaker of rum. It had all gone so well; he was delighted with Abby's family and proud of his own. But there was a shadow on Abigail's brow; small and light though she was, she was a leaden weight to his lifting, and she begged him to put her down. He drew her outside to the bench by the door, so they could talk without listeners.

At first she would not tell him what it was that had dis-turbed her. "Something my sister said, perhaps?" Joel in-sisted.

Abby swallowed hard. "She presumes—as if it were only natural—that I will become a Jewess. . . . Did *you* think it too, Joel?"

"I—" Joel's heart sank; he knew he had not faced this. "Well, I did not much think of it, I'm afraid. Women do usually take the faith of their husbands, isn't it true?"

"Not always," she said. "I know some, right here in Fair-field, who married Jews, and their husbands have joined the Church. Why not you, Joel?"

167

There was pathetic, desperate pleading in Abigail's voice, but Joel drew away, outraged. "Surely you did not think that I would convert?"

Abigail's distress was visibly mounting. "Haven't you said, often, that it is the same God we worship, in two different ways?"

"Yes, I said that."

"Then why should you refuse to change your *way* of worship, when you know it means so much to me?"

He took her hand, struggling to explain his feeling in a manner that would not offend her own. "There are many shades of difference in what we believe, my dearest—and one big difference. To me, Jesus was a great man—one of the greatest of all time. If the words he preached were followed, there would no longer be wars between men of different nations, races or sects. He also was a Jew, remember? Much of Christianity stems from his Judaism—why then should I oppose it? But I do not believe that he was the Messiah; Jesus is not my Lord and my Redeemer."

Abigail pulled her hand away and got up. "But that is what a heathen thinks!" She walked a few steps from him and turned her back, gazing out at the drab November fields in the fading light of afternoon. Seen thus, stiff and silent, she could have been her own mother, a Puritan, strict, stubborn and uncompromising.

A sense that his love was doomed came upon Joel, and a wild childish wish that everything they had said in the last minutes could be wiped out. He was bitterly hurt, yet he could not be angry with Abigail because he knew she was feeling the hurt too. It was chilly now that night was falling;

168

he fetched her scarlet cloak from the peg inside the door and gently put it round her shivering shoulders. At the light touch of his hands, she turned and flung her arms around him, with the tears running down her face. "Oh Joel, Joel, we must not quarrel! Over this or any other thing. You are far too dear to me!"

"You're cold, dear Abby, and overtired by all that has happened today," he said. "We'll go inside and talk no more about it for this evening. Surely we can find a way to settle this."

But a blight had fallen upon them; the question was in the back of their minds no matter what else they spoke of. Abigail begged him to come to Meeting with her on the Lord's Day, so that he could see what it was like. "We have been building a new Meeting House, more beautiful than the one that burned. It means—oh, I cannot tell you all that it means to me. While you, by your own admission, have not entered the house of your God in many a day."

"There was no synagogue near for me to go to while I was in the army," Joel said, "but whenever there were ten of us who could gather to pray on the Sabbath together, we did so."

To please her, he went on the following Sunday to the half-finished church in Green's Farms, where the simple services, the heartfelt singing of the Psalms, the prayers for peace and freedom, made him feel more than ever that it was one God whom both he and Abby worshiped. But, he told her, he could not join this church and so become a professing Christian. "Perhaps, dear heart," he said, "you can continue to attend your kind of holy services and I mine." She nodded, but he felt she was not satisfied. Nor was he. Both knew they would have to talk it out further.

Mistress Bailie brought up the question of the marriage ceremony.

"I have always dreamed of the day when our dear parson, who has known me since I was little, would hear my marriage vows," Abby said.

"There are words in your marriage ritual which I cannot say," Joel objected.

"Oh Joel, you are so stiff-necked!" Abigail said.

"There will be many things more difficult to deal with than words," Squire Bailie reminded them. "And it is quite customary here in Connecticut to be married by a magistrate."

"Very well, then, let it be a civil ceremony," Abby said, and smiled at Joel.

For the moment they were glad, but the peace did not last for long. The following afternoon, which was raw and cold, with the wind still blowing, they were sitting on the settle, warming their feet before the fire. Squire Bailie and Gurdon were from home, and Mistress Bailie was busy in the next chamber. Joel stared into the flames and said, "It is almost as cosy as if we were sitting by our own hearth. It will be good to be together at last, we two alone, won't it?"

Abigail fell in with his mood. "But I will be a busy house-wife then, with too many chores to sit and moon with you all afternoon."

"Naturally. There will be my socks to mend—clothes to make. And children to feed—" he added, teasing.

She bowed her head and the scarlet mantled her cheeks. "Then, before I put the children to bed, I will have to hear their catechism—" She looked up at him with startled eyes. "You did not intend that our children should be raised in the Jewish faith?"

"I surely do not intend them to be Gentiles," he replied sharply.

"But Joel—this—this I could not permit! This I could not bear—that my children should not be true believers on Christ—"

"Oh Abby, Abby," he said sadly. "Do you not remember Ruth, who said, 'Thy people shall be my people, and thy God, my God'?"

"Yes, but I am not Ruth."

"No, you are not Ruth," he said. "I was a fool to expect it."

"Joel—" she began pitifully. Before she could say more there was a loud pounding at the door. Joel found Denis standing there. "Major Tallmadge wants you, Joe. Better come quick; he's impatient."

"I will be with you on the instant," Joel said. He snatched his hat from the peg, started for the door, looked back for a moment at Abigail, standing before the hearth, her hair lit up like a bright halo. Her hands were clasped as if begging; her eyes were big and unhappy, but her small mouth was firmly pressed together.

"Good-by, Abigail," Joel said. "I will return when I can."

17.

"I AM glad you are prompt," Major Tallmadge said, as Joel entered the room in the house which served as temporary headquarters. "Captain Barry tells me the storm is letting up and that we should be able to embark by tomorrow. Meanwhile there is much to do."

His manner was military and formal, although he and Joel had come to know each other well. Wax tapers, flickering in the gusty wind that still rattled the windows, made his tall, erect shadow leap on the plastered wall, and molded his frown of concentration with hollows and sharp high lights. He picked up a chart from the mass of papers on the desk. "Fort St. George is on the Great South Bay, a good fifteen miles from our probable landing place. That will be a long march through country infested with Loyalists. You know, of course, why its capture is of importance?"

"It's a supply depot, isn't it?" Joel said.

"Not only that. It is the most eastern of the British fortifications on Long Island. By destroying it, we shall break up the enemy's spy system between their posts on the Island and Tory sympathizers here. And also make well-nigh impossible the Tory raids which have plagued these shores. Then, for the first time in five years, our good New England folk will be free to give wholehearted assistance to the Army elsewhere."

He smoothed out some sheets of paper, closely written in the ink stain which was invisible till properly treated. "According to these messages from my spies, the place is heavily fortified and well garrisoned. Till now, General Washington was unwilling to let me undertake such a risk. I have managed to persuade him, but it is a grave responsibility. Everything depends on surprise. Here is a sketch of the fort and stockade." He pointed with a quill. "As you see, it will not be easy to take. You are to warn the men under you of this."

"The entire detachment has been carefully picked, sir, as you know—I don't think you'll find any fainthearted fellows."

"We shall need a number of axes with which to cut down the stockade; you will see to collecting them before tomorrow."

"I will attend to it, sir."

"That is all for tonight." He smiled, dropping the role of commanding officer. "Now, Joel, will you join me in a glass?"

"Gladly," Joel said.

"You seem troubled, my boy," the major said, as he poured out the Madeira. "You will acquit yourself well to-

173

morrow, I know—you have never failed me so far. What is it that disturbs you?"

Joel gazed into his glass as if it were a crystal ball in which he could read the future. "It's—well, I am very puzzled over something. Because you were born in America, maybe you could understand it better than I do—if you can spare a moment?"

"A moment is possible among friends, even in wartime," Tallmadge said, sipping his wine.

"It is like this—" Joel told what had happened in the last few days between himself and Abigail. "And so we love each other, but we do not agree on this one thing. And I don't know what can be done about it."

"Your Abigail is not being unreasonable in this," Tallmadge said. "The Church is very important to us New Englanders; our forefathers planned this colony to be a little model of the glorious kingdom of Christ on earth, and it was for this they came here and suffered in the wilderness. To desert our faith, even for love, would be treachery both to God and country."

"And I feel the same," Joel said. "My belief also is too dear to change—even for love." He put down his glass. "I will see about the axes now, sir. Thank you and good night."

He was glad there was to be action tomorrow. He did not know what he could say to Abigail, and he feared that if he spoke further with her, the rift between them would deepen.

Next day the wind had dropped somewhat, though the Sound was still lead gray under an angry sky. Tallmadge's dragoons and the whaleboat crews that were to transport them

—slightly under a hundred men in all—waited on the bleak beach, shivering and idly watching the flocks of gulls which wheeled in the sky and bobbed among the waves as if gathering for some expedition of their own. The cold, the gloom, the still angry sea, the gulls calling like frightened children, were not such things as made the men feel there would be a happy outcome to this raid. They knew of too many others that had failed, with boats lost, men killed and captured by British sloops of war. But the boat crews, hard-bitten Yankees used to the dangerous trade of whaling, joshed one another.

"Brisk weather for crabbing, ain't it?" said one.

"There ain't enough meat on blue claws for my taste," said another, a lean old fellow with a nutcracker face. "I'm setting my trap for Lobsters."

"Thought you'd be shy of Lobsters at your age, Pop," said one of the dragoons. "This place we're going is fortified like Ticonderoga, Major says."

"Fortyfied or not, didn't we take Fort Ti in '75?" answered the old man. " 'Course we lost it again later, but them generals always fumble when we leave it up to them."

"Time to go, boys," Captain Matt Barry cut in. The whitecaps had subsided somewhat and Tallmadge had given the order to embark. Already he had delayed so long that Tory spies might have got word across to the enemy.

The November day was drawing to a close; darkness would be a good cover, and the wind was fair for Long Island. In Matt Barry's boat, the mast had been taken from under the benches and set up; the sail bellied out, and the men rowed with slow strokes, for they had miles of tumbled water to cross. The long heavy boat climbed up over the swells and dropped with a slap and splash into the trough; spray flew, harsh and icy. Joel plunged his raw knuckles deeper into the pockets of his tow-cloth coat and drew the scarf Abby had knitted him close about his neck. Clouds scudded before the wind; somewhere, unseen, a big fish leaped, and a covey of sea birds swooped by with high lost crying. Denis' very voice sounded green as he said, "Was it a f-favor you thought you was doing, Joe me boy, when you persuaded the major to let me join his company? Begorra, till now I never knew what a s-saint St. Patrick was to cross the sea for the converting of the Irish!"

Enough spray had come in over the bow to make a chill puddle underfoot which slopped back and forth as the boat wallowed and yawed before the wind. To be both cold and seasick seemed the utmost in misery. Joel himself felt no squeamishness, but Denis had plenty of company; many of Tallmadge's dragoons were clutching their stomachs, groaning, or leaning over the side. The night was black as a coalpit; they could neither see the other boats nor hear voices from them above wind and wave. An occasional distant eerie halloo cheered them with the hope that they were not alone in the underworld on the Styx, the river of the Dead. The four hours of crossing seemed like a lifetime: as if they would never see the sun rise again.

Matt Barry, standing in the stern with his long steering oar, gave a short grunt of satisfaction. Straining his eyes, Joel managed to make out high bluffs sloping to a beach which gleamed faintly pale. "The Old Man's, that beach is called," Matt said. "Futher east than we meant to come, but the major said to stay well away from Huntington, so this is it."

"And j-just the weather for a long walk," Denis chattered, as a sudden gust of wind lifted a corner of the sail.

The keel of the boat nudged against sand. "Over the side, all of you," Captain Matt said. "There ain't apt to be look-outs here, but go quietly as you can just the same."

As well ask horses or cattle to tread lightly; the sloshing of so many feet through the shallows started up a hoarse scolding mud hen from the reeds. If there were enemies on this seemingly deserted shore, they'd not be in any doubt of what was happening. The other boats were coming in one after another, discharging their passengers and being pulled up on the beach by their crews as soon as empty. And again the men were standing around a beach waiting for orders, but now it was dark, and they were colder because wet, and the wind still blew.

"I don't like the smell of the weather," Matt Barry mut-tered to Joel. "Blowing from the east again." He shrugged, as if to say there was nothing to be done about it now.

Major Tallmadge strode across the sand. "Captain Barry, you will remain here with twenty of the crew to guard the boats. If it looks as though we are delayed, hide them in the marsh grass as best you can." To Joel he said, "Muster your men in for the march, Sergeant."

Matt shook Joel's hand. "Good luck, boy. We'll be watch-ing for you."

Behind the beach was a maze of creeks and tidal pools and bogland, rough and wet underfoot. The men squelched through mud; staggered over hummocks and pitched into holes unseen in the dark. "By Glory," said a tall dragoon, "I thought the major had us dismounted to be Rangers, not haddock and flounder!"

"You have been sitting a horse so much, you have forgotten how to use those long legs of yours," Joel said; "don't blame the major for it."

The dragoon laughed. "Oh, I warn't blaming, just remarking. I'd do most anything for Ben Tallmadge."

Beyond the marsh they climbed upward through a tangle of shriveled vines and bushes which failed to cut off the wind beating about their ears or give shelter from the rain which was beginning to fall. The Sound was whipping up again; they could hear the waves crashing on the beaches. To be caught in this territory, unable to return because of the gale, would be disastrous; it was a rattlesnake nest of Tories and British Regulars. Yet if they retreated across the Sound now, to avoid the worst of the storm, this opportunity to surprise the British might never come again.

Major Tallmadge ordered the column to right-about-face and return to the shore. A groan went up, for his men were eager for action. Then word passed that they would stay close to the beach till the weather cleared, hoping not to be discovered there.

For the rest of the night they hid in the scanty shelter of scrub pines and scraggy bushes, like a flock of lost sheep huddling together for warmth. They did not dare to warm themselves with a fire. Some, lighthearted as Denis, curled up to sleep. Joel could not sleep, but lay listening to the monotonous patter of the cold rain on the soggy bed of leaves, thinking of many things.

When he thought of Abby, instead of it bringing happiness, as it used to, the thought was a sore spot in his breast. In spite of what Major Tallmadge had said, he did not believe that she could really love him if she could not accept his faith for herself and their future children. Joel's Jewishness was a vital part of him; without it he was nothing. One as well read in the Bible as Abigail must remember the words of the Psalm: "If I forget thee, O Jerusalem, let my right hand forget her cunning. If I do not remember thee, let my tongue cleave to the roof of my mouth; if I prefer not Jerusalem above my chief joy." Joel's love for Abby had been his chief joy throughout the struggles and hardships of the last year. But he could not give up the doctrine for her, nor allow his children to be deprived of its heritage, a belief in the importance of peace, justice and freedom, no matter what the cost to the individual.

It was this that made Joel wish he had been more in the thick of things. Five years had passed since the Declaration of Independence, since the day when he had cried, "If this is truly meant, then this is my country!" For the Patriot Army it had been five years of retreating, of stubborn resistance, of big defeats and only small successes. Why then did he hope, why did they all go on hoping? Because we *have* to win, he told himself; anything else was unthinkable.

For him the war had been four fifths waiting and the other fifth little raids like this one. When the big events took place, he was always somewhere else: Bunker Hill had found him in jail; during the Battle of Brooklyn, he had been standing on the wrong side of the river; when Burgoyne had surrendered at Saratoga, he had been battling insects in the Bailies' garden.

Once when he had accused himself in this fashion, Denis had said to him, "You've fought plenty, Joe. You Jews just take things too all-fired hard!"

"Yes," Joel had answered soberly, "I guess we do." Many young Jews were taking this war hard; he heard tales of them among the soldiers: of "the Jew Davis," killed in '76; "the Jew Franks," captured at Brooklyn, and "that surgeon's mate at Valley Forge—Russell—did you know he was a Jew?" Bush, Hays, Levy, Cohen—Joel ticked off the names on his fingers—one could go on and on.

He rolled over on his back and stared at the dripping twigs, lacy against the first gray of morning. The branches shifted and chattered; the pines swayed in the wailing storm wind. Joel shivered, trying to throw off the weight of oppression in his heart. It was stupid to lie here, unable to sleep, tiring himself out when he needed to be fresh and alert for the coming raid. Maybe this was the time he wouldn't come back; Abby would mourn him as a hero for a little while, and that would be that. No, by Heaven, he was no weakling to think of death as a solution for difficulties. Somehow he'd figure out a solution for himself and Abigail, but it would have to wait. First there was the problem of the raid on Fort St. George.

All day the storm wind blew, while the men crouched among the leaves, expecting to be flushed from the shelter like partridges by Tory hunters. They dared not even talk. Anyone who coughed or sneezed got the dirty looks due a traitor. Toward evening the wind and rain stopped at

180

last, and Major Tallmadge gave the order to advance as soon as it was dark. Then the stamping of numb feet, the beating of cramped arms was loud enough to give any enemy within earshot warning. The tall dragoon said, "How'd you like to be me now, Sergeant? The longer the leg, the more room there is for aches and pains and rheumatiz."

"I have enough trouble of my own, thank you," Joel grinned. The cold and wet had made his old leg wound ache; it always did in such weather.

They slugged across the Island through the night, across miles of flat pine barrens, along muddy roads and through thickets of bramble and pin oak where the few remaining leaves rattled like skeletons. At three in the morning Tallmadge ordered a halt and an hour's rest. While the tired men flopped on the ground, he summoned a council of war.

"We are now just two miles from the fort," he said. "I shall divide the men into three groups, each under an officer, and each to keep concealed till my group is discovered. Then we will attack from three directions at once. Sergeant Davidov will precede me with the pioneers and axes to beat down the obstructions. I will come close after. Do you all understand? Remember the watchword!"

It was four in the morning. The clouds had blown away and a few stars pin-pointed the sky, pale blue before dawn. The air was raw and chill, smelling of fish and clam flats. The land was low, sandy and flat, treeless and with none of Connecticut's boulders or stone walls for hiding places. Joel knew that if he led his men through the shoulder-high marsh grass, dried and brittle at this season, they would make as much noise as a herd of cattle. So he kept the company to a

181

narrow sandy road at the end of which could be seen, as daylight spread, the gleaming shallows of South Bay. Beyond this, on the dunes of the outer beach, Atlantic combers boomed in a steady rhythmic ebb and flow. Directly ahead a solid bulk with serrated edges loomed dimly against the sky: the stockade of Fort St. George.

Joel waved his men forward. They circled round, creeping almost on all fours, till the fort was scarcely forty yards away.

"Who comes there?" cried a sentry, firing even as he challenged.

"Sliver him!" cried someone in the American ranks, and before the smoke cleared, the Britisher had been bayoneted.

Joel, sprinting ahead, yelled, "Come on!" and the men charged, whooping and brandishing their axes as if they were tomahawks. In no time they had hacked the barred gate of the stockade to splinters and were surging with Tallmadge and his company across the parade ground to the main fort. On three sides the Americans had mounted the ramparts and were pouring in. From the three corners of the stockade, ringing voices cried out triumphantly the watchwords: *"Washington and Glory!"*

The startled garrison of the fort tried to defend themselves hand to hand against bayonet thrusts. Joel laid about him with his ax, since he had no other weapon. In less than ten minutes the commandant of the fort was crying for quarter; it was all over without a musket being fired. The surprise had done it!

The Americans gathered in the center of the enclosure, congratulating each other, slapping each other on the back

182

and joking about this easy success. Some of them squatted and some stretched out to ease their tired limbs. Joel remained standing, counting over his men. None were missing. Dawn was coming up, the promise of a golden autumn day, something to please the soul after the many days of storm. Joel stood breathing in the morning air, savoring in advance the warm sunshine that was to come. He took off his hat the better to enjoy it, and the morning breeze made his red hair stand up like a cock's comb.

From one of the two blockhouses at the corners of the stockade the crack of a musket sounded. "Why, the dirty varmints—firing after the commandant's struck his colors!" Denis cried. All of the Americans were shouting threats and picking up the weapons they had laid down.

Joel looked up at the window from which the shot had come, and he saw a face at the aperture, a long-jawed, thin-lipped face, a yellow sneering face . . . Alf Hodges. This fort was headquarters for Tory companies made up of renegade patriots; Joel might have guessed that Hodges would be here. Once he had spared this man's life, left him free to spread his poison of blind hatred, prejudice and treachery against his fellow man. If he went on living, who knows how many others he might infect with it? Joel grabbed the musket from Denis' hand.

But he had hesitated too long, a new volley of fire poured down on the parade ground. Joel put his hands to his head and staggered. Everything around him was whirling in a red mist of pain. Denis ran to catch him as he fell.

183

18.

JOEL knew only darkness and throbbing pain. He did not know what had happened or where he was, nor did he care, at first. After days and nights that were blanks and others of scattered semiconsciousness, he knew that he was lying on something soft. It could not be the ground, and he was not dead in Heaven, Hell, or a cold grave. Smooth sheets covered his aching limbs. He put weak fingers to the eyes that could not see and touched a bandage. Perhaps the bandage was the reason he could not see.

A soft little hand took his own away from the bandages. A voice murmured something soothing. A familiar voice which he was glad to hear, though he could not remember why. He drifted off again.

Memory and understanding came back bit by bit. Now he was awake for several hours at a stretch, knew that he was Joel Davidov, that the hand and the voice were Abigail's.

He recognized other voices after a while: Abby's mother, urging him to take soup and gruel; Squire Bailie's, and Gurdon's, awkward and determinedly cheery.

At first he was too weak to question anything, but after a time the terrible question had to be asked. Already his hearing had grown keen, and he noticed the little catch of breath before Abby answered, "Of course you'll be able to see again. Only have patience."

The surgeon came; Joel said, "Tell me the truth. I am not a baby to be coddled."

"The truth is we do not know," the surgeon answered. "You have received a severe head wound which has affected your eyesight."

Joel interrupted him. "Permanently—so that I will always be blind?"

"We do not know," the doctor repeated. He had a kind voice, and it was a kind hand that rested for a moment on Joel's thin shoulder. "Don't despair, lad. You asked for a straight answer and I gave it to you, but I am not without hope for a happy outcome. In a few weeks we will take off the bandages; then we will know. Now you must lie still and recover from the shock of the blow."

Matt Barry came to sit by his bedside; told him, while Joel dozed and only half heard, the outcome of the expedition. Much ammunition and shipping and many stores destroyed at the British fort and hundreds of tons of forage at Coram as well; seven of the enemy garrison killed and many prisoners taken. Major Tallmadge had been well pleased.

"Any Americans killed?" Joel asked.

"Not even wounded—except for you. Our boys killed that

185

fellow who started the firing after the colors had been struck
—they'd've murdered all the Britishers in the blockhouse if
they hadn't been stopped."

Joel shrugged. He didn't care about being revenged. He
didn't even care much that Alf Hodges was dead. There
ought to be some better method for curing the disease of
hatred than by killing those who spread it.

Matt, watching Joel's gloomy, abstracted air, said, to
cheer him, "Things are going better in the rest of the country at last."

"How so?"

"Them Britishers have been taking a terrible licking in the
South. I tell you it looks like we're winning at last."

Joel was silent.

"Ain't you pleased?"

"Of course I am pleased."

"But you're miffed at missing out on the fun of being on
the winning side, ain't you? Everyone will jump on the band-
wagon now, but you kept fighting while the going was bad."
He slapped his knee. "By gravy, I come near forgetting to
give you a message from Ben Tallmadge—I was to tell you
that General Washington was mighty pleased about that
raid. Congress even passed one of those high-sounding resolu-
tions praising it."

"I'm glad Major Tallmadge got recognition," Joel said
wearily.

"One more thing, and then I'll leave you rest. The major
said to thank you for your end of the job—he's putting you
in line for a new decoration that's to be given only to common
soldiers and noncoms. Now ain't you proud?"

186

"Yes, I will be proud if I receive such a thing."

When Matt Barry had gone, Joel lay thinking. He had no right to be so angry and bitter at fate. He had not given his life for his country like Nathan Hale. But he did not particularly want his life without eyes to see the world about him, without eyes to see Abigail's face, without eyes to read the wisdom of the great books. Had he lost a limb, he could still have been a schoolmaster. Without sight, what could he do but be a burden to others? All the medals in the world, all the praise couldn't make up for that.

It was hard to lie still with these questions unanswered. Hour after hour he gripped the bed frame to keep from tossing, to lie quietly as the surgeon had ordered. He listened to the ticking of the clock and the crackle of the fire, and he felt the warmth of it, for his bed was drawn up close to the hearth in the kitchen. He heard the wind howling over the marshes and the sleet beating against the windows. At first he had slept constantly; now he slept hardly at all, and the nights were long.

So were the days, but there was Abigail's presence to shorten them. He would listen for her light step as she flew about her household tasks; the tap of her foot on the treadle as she sat by his side spinning. She was gentle with him save when she scolded him for being gloomy. "Of course everything is going to be all right with you," she said. "As soon as you are well enough to be out of bed, we will post the betrothal notices."

Short-tempered these days, he snapped at her, "So you wouldn't marry a whole Jew, but you would marry a blind one—out of pity. No thank you!"

187

"I never said I wouldn't marry you!" she cried indignantly, and ran from the room. He thought he heard a muffled sob.

She had not *said* she would not marry him, but Joel was sure it had been in her mind to say so that evening before he had left for the raid. Nevertheless he called to her, "Abigail —dear Abby—come back!"

She knelt by his side, burying her head against the coverlet. He stroked her soft hair, passed his fingers over her face. "No, Abby, I can't let you marry a helpless cripple, even if we manage to figure out our other difficulties. Have you forgotten them?"

"No—but I won't let them get in the way. I'm going to marry you anyhow, no matter how you deny me," Abigail answered with her old defiance.

"Have I no say in it?" he smiled.

"None at all. You don't know what's good for you."

"Supposing I don't want such a domineering wife?" he teased.

She kissed his cheek; he reached to embrace her and found her tense and trembling. He dropped his arms. "Ach, what a lot of fuss about a little damage. I'll be able to see as well as anyone probably, when this stupid bandage is off." But he did not believe it. And he would not marry Abby if he was blind.

Slowly he grew stronger till he was allowed to sit up. Gurdon helped him with his clothes, delighted to be of use. He took a few steps, leaning on the boy's arm. The surgeon said he would remove the bandages soon; after Christmas, he said.

Joel did not care about Christmas; it was not a day for him

188

to celebrate. He was reminded that *Hanukkah*, the Feast of Lights, would soon be at hand, and he was seized with a fierce longing to observe it with a Jewish family. It had been such a long time since he had enjoyed any festival with his own kind; even during the High Holy Days of autumn, he had been in the army among Gentiles.

The surgeon refused to allow Joel to travel as far as New Haven, but he relented when Joel pleaded for Norwalk instead. "Let someone drive you carefully in a wagon," he said.

Joel agreed. There was no Jewish community in Fairfield, but he remembered the many Jewish faces he had seen in Norwalk. He asked Gurdon, as a favor to him, to search out a family by the name of Levino there and inquire if Joel Davidov might be with them on the first *Hanukkah* evening.

When the date came, Abigail pleased Joel by asking if she might go with him. Matt Barry brought round a wagon filled with straw and warm blankets and drove the two of them over the frosty roads to Norwalk. Abigail guided Joel to the house door, and when it opened, his hands were taken in a warm clasp and Judith Levino's voice welcomed him. Warned beforehand by Gurdon, she said nothing about his bandaged eyes. "We are honored to have you with us," she told Abigail. They were surrounded by welcoming voices: Judith's aunt and uncle, other kinsfolk, friends and children. Many children, big and little, according to the giggles and squeaks of excitement. Sweetmeats and presents were thrust on Joel, and he was drawn to a comfortable chair with Abigail beside him. He could tell by her voice that she felt awkward, as he had when he had first come from Poland. Now it was Abby who was the stranger, while to him the surroundings were so familiar that he could picture them without eyes. The smell of the cake and goodies was familiar, and the pungent odor of the pine boughs with which the room was decorated. He did not need eyes to see the big brass candle-holder, old and well-polished, and the eight tall tapers in it.

"Hush, little ones," said Judith's uncle. "I am going to read to you from the Book of Maccabees. But first, to honor the lady who is our guest, I tell a little in English." He smiled at Abigail, seated very erect and prim and a bit nervous, by Joel's side. "The story happened in our year of three thousand, five hundred and ninety-three—that would be one hundred and sixty-eight years before the birth of your Jesus. The Syrian tyrant had conquered all Judea and set up heathen idols in our Holy Temple. The Jews revolted, of course, and after a while Judah the Maccabee—a great hero—and his men came down from hiding in the hill caves above Jerusalem to set the people free. After the battles, when the Syrians were driven out, Judah went to cleanse the Temple. He found there only one cruse of oil that had not been defiled. When he rekindled the sacred lamp, the oil from that single vessel didn't last just a day, but for eight days!"

He picked up a book in worn leather binding and read from it in Hebrew. Then he kindled a paper spill at the fire and gave it to little Sara, that she should light the first of the candles.

Joel, singing *Mo-oz Tzur*, Rock of Ages, with the others, felt his hope and spirit lift. He still had his faith, and a voice with which to spread those things in which he believed.

"What does it mean?" Abigail whispered, when the sing-

ing of the *Hanukkah* hymn was ended. Joel told her the
words of the last verse in English:

> "Yours the message cheering
> That the time is nearing
> Which will see
> All men free,
> Tyrants disappearing.

"Each night for eight nights we light one more candle till
they are all kindled," he said. "It is so we remember how our
forefathers fought once for their homes, for God, and for
liberty; how we must always do this." Even if it kills or
cripples us, he thought, but was suddenly no longer so bitter.

As they drove homeward under a sky sparkling with stars,
Abigail said wonderingly, "It was like Independence Day; it
was beautiful, Joel—and the people were so kind."

"I am glad you liked them," Joel said.

"The young girl—Judith Levino—was friendly, but she
stared at me so! I wonder why—has she never seen a Christian?"

Joel laughed. "I am *quite* sure that she has, since she was
born and brought up in this country. I suppose she was
curious that a Puritan maid should come to a Jewish festival.
Should I have told her why you have a special interest?"

"No, no," said Abigail hastily, "it is just as well that we
keep it to ourselves till the banns are posted."

The visit had given Joel a measure of peace and hope. He
occupied his mind with planning how he might be able to
teach children even if it turned out that he was blind. He
had read much, and remembered it well; other books

could be read to him by kind friends. Already Abigail had the habit of reading aloud to him from a book of sermons.

"Here is one that should interest you," she said, rustling the pages. "It is by the Reverend Langdon, president of Harvard. This is what he says: 'The Jewish government, according to the original constitution, which was divinely established, was a perfect republic. . . . The civil policy of Israel is doubtless an excellent model, allowing for some peculiarities; at least some principal laws and orders of it may be copied in more modern establishments.' He says when the ancient Israelites had a king, it was punishment for their folly."

Joel chuckled. "Perhaps. But without King Solomon, we should have missed the most beautiful love song of all time."

"I do not believe King Solomon meant earthly love by what he wrote," Abigail said primly. She read on for several pages, closed the book, and poked him. "Joel! You are half asleep! When I try so hard to keep you amused."

He smiled lazily. "I know you do, dearest, and I'm grateful, believe me. I've been a burden on you too long; now that I'm better, I should go back to New Haven, to my own family."

"Not till the bandages are off from your eyes. And the surgeon said that could not be till after Christmastide."

In Fairfield, Joel found, the birth of Jesus was not celebrated with jollity and feasting, such as he had witnessed in the Old World. Such goings on smacked of pagan revelry, Mistress Bailie said; in her own childhood it had been a day of fasting, and even now the Bailie family observed it quietly with Bible reading and prayer. Peace on earth, good will to men—Joel could wholeheartedly join in prayers for such things as these. And yet—and yet there came awkward moments between himself and Abby, beliefs voiced by one and not by the other, subjects from which both backed away for fear of treading on the other one's toes. Yet to back away made Joel feel dishonest and disloyal; he was sure Abigail felt the same. He was tense and anxious in any case, though he tried not to show it, for soon he would know the final verdict on his sight.

The surgeon came to remove the bandages. And as the long strips of linen dropped away, the water came to Joel's eyes; the unaccustomed daylight hurt him, and the objects before him were blurred. But he could see! Soon, the doctor said, he would be able to see as well as ever. Only have patience, he advised, as he put back the bandages for a few days more. After that, he said, Joel could set off for New Haven if he wished.

Joel could have patience easily now. Now he could listen to the wind blow and know that soon again he would be able to see the grasses bending before it and the branches tossing; he felt a sunbeam on his face and dared to remember how it gilded the meanest object with its magic; he heard the hissing snow and pictured how white and candy-frosted each twig must be. "To love the world truly," he told Abigail, "everyone should be blind for a little while. Most especially those who revel in destroying what God has wrought."

He knew he should be happy now that the terrible threat to his future had been removed. He should be happy and full of plans. Instead, a sad lonesomeness was growing in him, and he did not let himself think beyond the next day.

When Squire Bailie spoke of posting the betrothal notices, both Joel and Abby put him off. Nor did they discuss this with one another.

After the surgeon had come again to remove the bandages, Joel told Abigail that he must be leaving soon. She sat for a moment with bent head. "God be praised, you are going to be entirely well again, Joel, aren't you?"

"Yes, Abby; I am quite well, even now."

She took a short breath. "We must speak of plans then."

He nodded, and took her hand in his. It was icy cold. "The time has come when we must be honest with one another." He hesitated. "You no longer wish to marry me, Abby, do you?" he said in a low voice.

"I wish to—if you would only become a Christian, Joel. There is so little difference—"

"So little," he said, with the pain rising in him so he could hardly speak. "So little, yet my answer is still the same. And yours is too—isn't it, Abby?"

"I love you as much as always," she said pitifully. "But I cannot desert my church—and you will not leave yours—"

"Some day people like us," he said drearily, "will be able to marry without betraying their God. I can't picture when or how, but I'm sure He cannot wish to keep apart always two who love each other and who both believe His ways are good. Only now—you and I haven't managed to find the way."

She held his hand tight, and they sat together while the winter sunlight faded from the room.

Joel and Abigail were alone for a last word together. Joel had said his good-byes to the rest of the family, feeling, in

Squire Bailie's firm handclasp, in his wife's sad smile, in Gurdon's stammering words of gratitude, the knowledge that they were deeply sorry to see him go. Outside the house, Matt Barry was waiting with his wagon to drive Joel to New Haven.

"I will never forget all the things you taught me, Joel," Abigail said, trying to smile.

"You too taught me much," Joel answered. Her clouded eyes, the sweet brave face he loved, the mouth he had kissed, filled him with a tenderness and a sense of loss almost unbearable. "Let's not forget, either, the happiness we had together—for we were happy most of the time, Abby, weren't we?"

"We were very happy, dear Joel." She covered her face with her hands. Gently he took her hands away and kissed her a last time. Then he walked out of the door to the waiting wagon.

19.

1783

JOEL strolled up Great Dock Street from the wharf where Matt Barry had at last found a spot in which to tie up his new trading sloop. The November day was clear, cold and brilliant. The bright sun sparkled on the East River and a keen nor'wester dashed the water into lacy froth against the sides of the rotting old prison hulks, abandoned now, and the long lines of British transports waiting to sail. The wind had delayed Joel's arrival, but he was just as well pleased, for he had reached New York on the great day—the day that was to see the last of the King's troops.

Marks of the British occupation were everywhere, but noon today had seen the end of it. The trampled gardens would be raked and weeded, and by spring they would be blooming neatly again; the shade trees, which had been cut down for soldiers' fires, would be replaced with saplings; already the churches that had been used as barracks and stables were being cleaned. Shells of houses destroyed by the great fire still supported canvas roofs which had sheltered the thousands of Tory refugees who had fled to the protection of this last British stronghold. Now these refugees had gone aboard the transports in the river, and the things they could not take with them—furniture, books, pictures, clothing, children's toys—were piled on the sidewalks to be sold at auction.

Today the streets seethed with the winning side; with holiday crowds, dressed in their best; Continental soldiers in the uniforms of their regiments, neat and clean, with buttons polished and faces shaved; militia men swaggering with jaunty feathered hats and broad grins, which boasted they could lick the whole world if they wanted to.

Joel too, as he walked along, was bursting with pride; not for himself alone but for his fellow countrymen—yes, now he dared to call them that. Although the war, to all practical purposes, had been over after the British surrender at Yorktown two years before, this was the day for which all Americans had been waiting.

He thought of all that had happened since he had left the house at Compo. He had gained back his strength slowly, in spite of his sister's coddling. "How do you expect to get well if you won't eat?" Miriam scolded. "To pine so after a girl —it's childish, Yosele!"

Maybe so, Joel thought, but it was months before he could think of Abigail without a knife twisting inside him. The curly red hair grew back over the scar on his skull and his eyes were as good as ever, but the surgeon said there was to be no more soldiering for him. He did not struggle against the doctor's verdict; his side was winning, and people were beginning to plan for the future. After a while, Joel too made his plans hopefully; peace was a business in which he had more of an interest than war. He had gone back to work for Jacob as his health improved, but he knew the world of commerce was not for him. The errand which had brought him to New York today might well be the last one he would do for his brother-in-law.

By now he thought of Abby only with tenderness and regret. This wound too had mended slowly and had left a scar, but healed it was at last. Abby had been part of his youth, part of his joy in his new country and his struggle to understand it. Eight years had passed since he had first seen her at New London; three since they had finally parted. He was twenty-five now, and he had learned to understand that he was both an American and a Jew, with loyalty to the democratic ideals which played so large a part in both traditions.

When Matt Barry told him Abby had married—"a solid lad, and a brave one, too"—Joel remembered that she had dreaded to become an ancient maid, and was glad for her sake. Denis also was settled down, with a New England lass for wife and a position in New London as Mr. Shaw's head clerk. As for himself, he sometimes thought his heart was frozen; perhaps he had been buffeted by too many winter winds. It would be a sad life with no children of his own to cheer him, yet since leaving Abby, no girl had seemed to him lovely or sweet.

He wandered on, deep in thought, to Mill Street, past the small plain building that was the synagogue, where the doors would soon again be open of a Sabbath. It's remarkable how we survive, he thought; we're used to wars, even though we hate them. He wondered where the Levino family was, and what had happened to young Judith.

For some time he had been conscious of distant cheering and the boom of salutes; now the squealing of the fifes was nearer, drums rolling in a frenzy, and martial music brassy loud above the people's shouting. From every street they were pelting toward Broad Way: stout merchants, beggars, seamen, dignified old gentlemen forgetting their dignity, goodwives and fine ladies holding up their skirts. There was such a press lining the avenue that Joel was obliged to mount a heap of rubble to see over the heads.

"Washington! Washington! Huzza for the Commander in Chief!" The roar of welcome came from the very hearts of the crowd, with the sound of adoration and thankfulness in it as well as triumph. Joel saw a tall gaunt man sitting very erect on a prancing gray horse, at the head of an escort of mounted officers and citizens. He looked old and worn, happy and very solemn. It was an ugly face, really, and yet a beautiful one. The crowd roared again. Joel felt a quiver run through him, and a lump came to his throat so that he could not cheer. The first time he had seen Washington— that dreadful day on the Brooklyn shore—how different things had been!

He put his hand in his pocket and fingered (smiling at himself for his pride in it) a carefully folded, heart-shaped piece of purple silk edged with lace which he carried there, since he no longer wore a uniform. And in his own heart he carried the Commander in Chief's orders conferring the decoration: *"Not only instances of unusual gallantry, but also of extraordinary fidelity and essential service in any way shall meet with a due reward. . . . Men who have merited this distinction to be suffered to pass all guards and sentinels which officers are permitted to do. The road to glory in a patriot army and free country is thus open to all. . . ."* Well, Joel didn't think he had done anything extraordinary, but he had done his best. And now, God be praised, the war was over.

The procession had passed by; Joel descended from his perch, jostled by the crowd that was dispersing to homes and taverns. A hand touched his shoulder and a voice shouted in his ear, "Joel Davidov! Now at last we can truly say *Shalom* —it is peace!"

"David Levino!" Joel cried joyfully. "I heard you were a prisoner in England."

"So I was. But they grew tired of me, and I was exchanged in time for the last of the Southern campaigns."

"You were lucky," Joel said. "And the rest of your family —are they still abroad?"

"Only Rachel, who married the heir of an English banking family, which is just what she wanted." He stepped back to examine Joel. "You look healthy enough. Didn't I hear that you were badly wounded?"

"It seemed so at the time, but I'm recovered, as you see," Joel said. "How did you hear it?"

"From my little sister Judith—have you forgotten her?"

"Of course not—she and your kinsfolk were very kind to me in Norwalk. But I didn't think she would have mentioned

200

the bandage with which I was decorated that *Hanukkah* evening."

"She mentioned more than that; she seems to think highly of you." David linked his arm affectionately through Joel's. "Have you a place to stay tonight?"

"Not yet. I am going to a tavern—"

"You'll never find a bed in a tavern on a night like this. I'm afraid you'll have to put up with one in our house again."

"Your father hardly welcomed me the last time I asked for shelter," Joel said with sarcasm he could not hide.

"I know it. He told me so with shame. He's an old man and timid, my father. Don't hold it against him, Joel."

Joel found it hard to forgive Simon Levino's behavior to himself and especially to his wounded friend. Even though he understood it, he was not eager to accept hospitality from such a man.

"You would be doing all of us a great favor if you will forget the past," David Levino urged. "My father has said many times over how much he regrets turning you away. He was half-crazed with fear, as were many after that Brooklyn disaster. Besides which, I'd like a chance to talk with you, as would—other members of the family."

So Joel went along with David, agreeing that it was foolish to harbor resentment now that peace had come, and accepted Simon Levino's apologies when the merchant greeted him, with Mistress Levino, at the house door. Standing by the window of the parlor, looking out, was a young woman whom Joel took to be Rachel, forgetting for the moment that she had remained in England. This girl was taller than Rachel and more full-bodied, with a slim waist and a deep bosom.

Her gown was so simple that Rachel would have scorned it, and she wore no jewels but the tiny pearls in her ears. At the sound of the greetings, she turned and a smile lit up her rather serious face, oval and smooth-skinned—like cream with just a touch of coffee in it, Joel thought.

"Joel Davidov—how glad I am to see you again!" she said.

"Little Judith!" he cried astonished.

"*Little* Judith!" The violet eyes could twinkle. "You always call me little Judith, and you must admit I'm as tall as you are, now."

"Only because of the heels on those stylish slippers our sister sent you," David put in, to take her down a peg.

"That day, after Tryon's raid, you were hardly more than a child," Joel said, marveling at how she had changed.

"An awkward child, very excited to meet a soldier fresh from battle," Judith agreed.

"And the next time we met, I couldn't see you," Joel said, staring so that she dropped her eyes. He flushed, realizing his bad manners.

"You'll have to excuse me, Joel, for a little while," David broke in. "General Washington's officers are meeting at the tavern to toast him on his arrival. I won't stay long; meanwhile I'm sure you will be well entertained."

And so once more Joel found himself in the paneled dining room, where Simon Levino spoke the grace, broke the bread and poured the wine. The lovely furniture was scarred with the marks of spurs, where the careless British officers had kicked their heels against it, and most of the silver was gone; otherwise it was much the same. Joel remembered how timid and out of place he had felt that first time, how unsure of himself. *He* had changed. Seven years was a long time, he thought, stealing a glance at Judith.

A while after they had eaten and were seated in the parlor, David came bursting in, his face glowing with excitement. "You should have seen it!" he cried. "I stood at the side of the room with the younger men and heard the toasts they drank —General Washington and his officers! One I shall always remember—'To the Vindicators of the Rights of Mankind in every quarter of the Globe!'"

"We must all remember it," Judith said, looking up from her bit of sewing.

"I tell you, there are things stirring!" David went on. "Have you heard, Joel, of the Bill for Establishing Religious Freedom which Mr. Jefferson has introduced in the Virginia Assembly? It makes sure that no man shall be compelled to support any religious worship, or shall suffer because of his religious opinions. They say it will surely be passed and copied throughout the nation. Mr. Jefferson is a great man, a great statesman!"

"Once all you talked of, David, was Thomas Paine, and now it is all Thomas Jefferson," Simon Levino said. "Well, well, you young people have more courage and enthusiasm— and more wisdom perhaps, than I. . . . My dear," he said to his wife, "I am weary. Let us retire."

David yawned. "I'm weary too. We left Harlem at dawn to escort the General here. It has been a long day."

"But I am still too excited to sleep," Judith said. "I should like to stay down here in the parlor a little while, Mama, to watch the celebration from the window."

"May I keep your daughter company, Mistress Levino?" Joel asked.

"If you wish. Do not stay too late, Judith."

When they had gone, Joel walked over to the window to watch by Judith's side. In every house along this usually sleepy street, windows glowed cheerily yellow. Beyond the steep-sided roofs, the night sky was rosy with the reflection of illuminated buildings on Broad Way, and every so often a rocket swished up to burst into stars and explosions. Judith shuddered, and then smiled. "I can't get over thinking it is guns."

"But it isn't, Judith," Joel said; "no more guns! Listen—" There were cheers mingled with the boom of the fireworks, and somewhere men's voices were singing the old Liberty Songs; drunken voices, but the distance softened and mellowed the sound.

"Oh Joel," Judith said, "are you as happy as I am?"

"How could I help it?" he answered. "Everything is going to be better from now on—for everyone, I hope, as well as for me."

"What will you do, now that the war is over?" she asked him.

So Joel told her that at the New Year he was to take up a position as schoolmaster in a new free school in Connecticut. "I won't be paid much, and it's not a position of importance— at least that depends on how you look at it," he said. "For me, it's what I most want to do, my chance to help spread the ideas in which I believe. And I'm very fond of children; I like the job of teaching."

"Could anything be more important?" Judith said softly.

"This country will become whatever our children and our grandchildren make of it. They must learn why we fought this Revolution—and that it was not easy to get freedom." She turned back to the window to watch urchins dancing around a bonfire at the end of the street; their giddy shadows capered across the cobbles. "How different it all is from the first time you came here," Judith said. "Do you remember?"

"I remember that even then—in spite of your father— you were on our side. You said, 'God send victory to General Washington!' And he needed your prayers!"

"I prayed for victory every night," Judith said, "but it took more than prayers to make the dream come true."

"Then you went off to Norwalk, stubborn Patriot that you were," Joel continued. "How long was it that you stayed there?"

"Quite a few years; I have only just returned."

"Your parents must have missed you severely."

"I honor my parents," Judith said, "but they didn't need me and my aunt did. She is frail and was unused to housework, but my uncle couldn't afford a maidservant when he fled from New York, leaving his business. So my aunt and I shared the cooking and cleaning and looking after the children."

"You weren't used to doing housework either, were you?" Joel said, picturing the trim maidservants who cleaned and polished and served the meals in the Levino household.

Judith laughed. "I like it. It is far more amusing to brew up a fine meal than to direct others to do it. And I like being needed; I also liked being with people who felt as I did about the war. After the raid there were many worse off than we were, and we helped care for them too."

Joel remembered how tender Judith had been with her young nieces that day he had met her among the smoking ruins of Norwalk, how gently she had guided his blind footsteps on the *Hanukkah* eve. She was only eighteen even now, younger than Abby had been when they had parted, but she seemed far older. She was a woman rather than a girl, warm and softhearted, and sturdy too, in spite of her upbringing.

"And you, Joel?" she said, turning away from the window, "are you quite all right again?"

"Oh yes. Of course I've a small limp, and a very fine scar on my head—in fact this body of mine is a crock, but it works well enough for my purposes."

She hesitated. "That pretty Gentile that was with you for *Hanukkah*—Abigail Bailie—how does she?"

"She's married, I'm told."

Judith gave a scarcely perceptible sigh. Then the warm pink came to her cheeks. "Joel—why do you stare so?"

"Because you are so beautiful," he said.

"Beautiful—I? Rachel is beautiful, and Abigail Bailie too, but I—I am not delicate or slender, as they are. And look at these hands," she stretched them out. "They are the hands of a charwoman, ugly, rough and red."

He took her two hands in his. It was true that they were not the smooth white hands of a gentlewoman; the nails had been trimmed short and callouses ran along the base of the fingers. "Beautiful hands," Joel said. "They have been properly used, your hands."

Her head, with the thick, lustrous dark hair was bowed;

206

her face was hidden, but she did not pull her hands away. With her hands in his, Joel was no longer alone. His heart was stirring from its winter sleep, and in it there was singing a verse from King Solomon's Song. But he dared not speak it aloud, not yet.

Then she lifted her face and looked at him as if she had heard him say it; her lips parted, as if to answer, but no sound came.

He raised her hands to his lips; her eyes, wet and violet blue as Sound water at sunset, flashed into his. And Joel knew that some day soon he would be able to tell Judith the words in his heart:

" 'Rise up, my love, my fair one, and come away. For, lo, the winter is past, the rain is over and gone; the flowers appear on the earth; the time of the singing of birds is come, and the voice of the turtle is heard in the land. . . .

" 'Arise, my love, my fair one, and come away.' "